I0600698

I Do, I Do, I Do

Robin Hawdon

A SAMUEL FRENCH ACTING EDITION

SAMUEL FRENCH

FOUNDED 1830

SAMUELFRENCH.COM
SAMUELFRENCH-LONDON.CO.UK

Copyright © 2013 by Robin Hawdon
All Rights Reserved
Cover Image © Gabriela Durán / Shutterstock

I DO, I DO, I DO is fully protected under the copyright laws of the United States of America, the British Commonwealth, including Canada, and all other countries of the Copyright Union. All rights, including professional and amateur stage productions, recitation, lecturing, public reading, motion picture, radio broadcasting, television and the rights of translation into foreign languages are strictly reserved.

ISBN 978-0-573-70107-8www.SamuelFrench.com

www.SamuelFrench-London.co.uk

FOR PRODUCTION ENQUIRIES

UNITED STATES AND CANADA
Info@SamuelFrench.com
1-866-598-8449

UNITED KINGDOM AND EUROPE
Theatre@SamuelFrench-London.co.uk
020-7255-4302

Each title is subject to availability from Samuel French, depending upon country of performance. Please be aware that *I DO, I DO, I DO* may not be licensed by Samuel French in your territory. Professional and amateur producers should contact the nearest Samuel French office or licensing partner to verify availability.

CAUTION: Professional and amateur producers are hereby warned that *I DO, I DO, I DO* is subject to a licensing fee. Publication of this play(s) does not imply availability for performance. Both amateurs and professionals considering a production are strongly advised to apply to Samuel French before starting rehearsals, advertising, or booking a theatre. A licensing fee must be paid whether the title(s) is presented for charity or gain and whether or not admission is charged. Professional/Stock licensing fees are quoted upon application to Samuel French.

No one shall make any changes in this title(s) for the purpose of production. No part of this book may be reproduced, stored in a retrieval system, or transmitted in any form, by any means, now known or yet to be invented, including mechanical, electronic, photocopying, recording, videotaping, or otherwise, without the prior written permission of the publisher. No one shall upload this title(s), or part of this title(s), to any social media websites.

For all enquiries regarding motion picture, television, and other media rights, please contact Samuel French.

MUSIC USE NOTE

Licensees are solely responsible for obtaining formal written permission from copyright owners to use copyrighted music in the performance of this play and are strongly cautioned to do so. If no such permission is obtained by the licensee, then the licensee must use only original music that the licensee owns and controls. Licensees are solely responsible and liable for all music clearances and shall indemnify the copyright owners of the play(s) and their licensing agent, Samuel French, against any costs, expenses, losses and liabilities arising from the use of music by licensees. Please contact the appropriate music licensing authority in your territory for the rights to any incidental music.

IMPORTANT BILLING AND CREDIT REQUIREMENTS

If you have obtained performance rights to this title, please refer to your licensing agreement for important billing and credit requirements.

CHARACTERS

ANN – 50ish, elegant

JAMIE – 30, her son, individual

HOLLY – 26, his sister, ditto

DIANA – 27, his bride-to-be, stunning

GEOFF – 30, his best man, good man

TOM – 30ish, his sister's boyfriend, ditto

SETTING

The main living room of a wealthy home on the outskirts of London. Superb, if showy, taste. Comfortable and expensive furnishings. Artistic adornments. On a shelf in a prominent position a reproduction statuette of Rodin's *The Thinker*. Upstage to one side a wide archway to the hall and the rest of the house. To the other side a door to the garden.

ACT ONE

SCENE ONE

(Afternoon. Sun pours in. **ANN** *is on the phone.)*

ANN. I know! Finally! Can you believe it! But listen, what I need to know from you is, will everything be all right on the day? Well are the stars propitious? Well you must be able to tell me something. There isn't going to be a tsunami or a volcano or anything? Not in Surrey, no not very likely. Well what about the weather at least? Silly question. Well can't you tell me *something*? It's going to be a very glamorous occasion. Yes, I know that – my husband keeps reminding me of the cost. It will all go splendidly – oh thank, you thank you! You see – that's all I wanted to hear. Talk to you soon – bye.

(Switches off. Waves a finger at The Thinker.*)*

See, I told you! He's never wrong. *(wavers)* Now…the shopping list. No…the raspberries.

(Goes off into the garden. The sound of a car. Door slams.)

HOLLY. *(calling off)* Hello – we're here.

(She enters with **TOM**. *They wear coats, he carries a weekend case. He gazes round.)*

TOM. Wow. Scary.

HOLLY. Don't be silly – it's just money. Bad taste really.

TOM. Superb taste.

HOLLY. Mother's of course. OTT. Meaning Ostentatiously Terrific Taste.

TOM. Very terrific.

HOLLY. She'll change it soon. This month Art Deco, next month Louis Quinze.

TOM. And Daddy lets her?

HOLLY. Oh, anything for peace. So long as he's piling in the bonuses.

(comes and clasps him)

Oh God, I do hope you like them all. Pretty bizarre family.

TOM. I'm sure not.

HOLLY. Well tricky. Look at me.

TOM. Yes, you're a nightmare.

(gives her a brief kiss)

So where are they all?

HOLLY. Oh, around. Except for Father. He'll be in Madrid or Frankfurt or somewhere, juggling billions.

(JAMIE *enters.*)

JAMIE. Oh, you're here. Thought I heard a car.

HOLLY. Here he is. The unblushing bridegroom. Jamie, this is Tom.

JAMIE. *(shaking hands)* Heard all about you.

TOM. Don't believe any of it.

JAMIE. No, not too bad actually. Want to watch yourself though if you're taking her on.

HOLLY. Thank you, sweetie – I love you too.

JAMIE. Lots of Michelin star dinners and a good spanking now and then – that ought to do it.

HOLLY. Isn't he insufferable?

TOM. I gather the wedding's in a month.

JAMIE. Yes. Terrifying thought.

TOM. Why?

JAMIE. We've been more-or-less together for four years, for Christ sake. Known each other most of our lives. What on earth do we want a posh wedding for?

TOM. So why…?

JAMIE. Parents' big day. Mother's chance to splash out. How could we deny her her fun?

HOLLY. Oh don't be such a wimp. Diana deserves a lovely wedding. *(to* **TOM***)* She's the most fabulous girl.

TOM. Diana.

HOLLY. Marshall. She could have had practically any man she ever met but she chose my plonky brother. He doesn't deserve her.

JAMIE. No, I don't, but there you are. Would you like a drink or something?

TOM. Bit early for me.

HOLLY. Cup of tea? You've driven all that way from London.

TOM. It's less than an hour – I'm fine. Do I get to meet the bride this weekend?

JAMIE. Oh I expect you'll meet everyone. She'll be round soon. Best man too. All curious to meet little sister's new man.

TOM. Oh hell.

JAMIE. Don't worry, they're quite tame. But we're one big family round here. Grew up together. Very country bumpkin incestuous.

TOM. *(looking round)* Hardly country bumpkin.

JAMIE. Well, no. They used to call it stockbroker belt. Now it's banker belt. And braces too.

TOM. Are you in banking also?

JAMIE. Good God no! Didn't she tell you?

TOM. I, er…We haven't known each other very long.

JAMIE. Long enough to get her into bed, I hope.

HOLLY. *(sighing)* Oh, Jamie…

JAMIE. Sorry. Prurient mind. No, I'm a bit of a lost cause so far. Tried academics, tried the law, tried PR. Sinking lower and lower – probably end up in politics.

TOM. What's wrong with banking?

JAMIE. I want to keep some friends.

TOM. Your father's done all right at it.

JAMIE. Yes, well you should never tread where a parent's trod. Shows you've no mind of your own. Though some would say I haven't.

HOLLY. He has, but it's a weird one.

JAMIE. You're an architect, I gather.

TOM. Yes. Struggling. Tough business unless you settle for lofts and renovations.

JAMIE. Well Mother will approve – gives you a head start. Play your cards right, she'll commission a new conservatory.

HOLLY. Where is she?

JAMIE. Um – three guesses. Garden, regimenting roses. Closeted with personal pilates instructor. On the internet ordering from Fortnums.

TOM. *(noticing the statuette)* Is that *The Thinker?*

JAMIE. Know your Rodins, do you?

TOM. If I could do that, I wouldn't need to be an architect.

HOLLY. Diana gave it to Jamie as a birthday present. Symbolising his passion for logic.

TOM. Logic?

HOLLY. Common sense, rationality. Great believer in rationality, aren't you Jamie? Just doesn't practise it very often.

JAMIE. Whereas Holly's a great believer in irrationality and practises it all the time. Like most women.

HOLLY. Sexist too. I told you we were a ghastly family.

JAMIE. Well, it's true. Mother won't embark on anything unless she's first consulted with her own personal astrologist. If that isn't irrational, I don't know what is.

(There is the sound of a male voice from the hall.)

GEOFF. Hello! Anyone at home?

HOLLY. That's Geoff. Best man. *(calls)* In the lounge! *(adds)* Like a brother really.

JAMIE. And there was a time when she wasn't averse to a spot of incest.

HOLLY. Bollocks. *(to* **TOM***)* I don't fancy him, I just love him. He keeps life exciting.

*(***GEOFF** *enters.)*

GEOFF. Ah – party's started.

HOLLY. *(hugging him)* Hello Geoff. This is Tom.

GEOFF. Ah. The latest.

TOM. *(raising eyebrows as they shake hands)* Oh. In a long line?

GEOFF. Hundreds. She's insatiable.

HOLLY. Geoff! You can go off people, you know.

GEOFF. You're the architect chap.

JAMIE. And frustrated sculptor.

GEOFF. Really?

TOM. No, not really.

GEOFF. Well it's high time she had somebody proper in fact. She's practically on the shelf.

HOLLY. You can *really* go off people! Anyway you can talk. *(to* **TOM***)* We're all beginning to think he's a poof.

GEOFF. Mmm, well…Hi, Jamie. Wedding still on, is it?

JAMIE. Just about. Big row brewing though.

GEOFF. Another one? What about?

JAMIE. Father's given Mother a list of fifteen business associates, together with wives, who he says just have to come. Nobody knows any of them but they're all highly important to our futures apparently.

GEOFF. Wow.

JAMIE. That'll put the numbers up to two hundred. Diana's parents will go berserk.

GEOFF. Does that mean I have to take the dirty bits out of my speech?

JAMIE. Oh no. The bigger the tycoon, the filthier the mind.

GEOFF. I'm thinking of the wives.

JAMIE. They're worse.

GEOFF. Right. Where is Diana?

JAMIE. I'm rather hoping she won't show up. I'll have to tell her.

GEOFF. Huge anticipation about this wedding, as you can tell, Tom.

TOM. Always tense occasions.

GEOFF. And this one's tense as a banker's bonus day.

(There is the sound of another car drawing up outside.)

Sounds like Diana's sporty motor now.

HOLLY. Let me show you your room, Tom. You'll want to freshen up before encountering the rest of the clan.

(leads him toward the door)

Do tell Mother we're here if she ever shows her face, Jamie.

JAMIE. Yes.

(They go off.)

He seems all right.

GEOFF. Is it serious?

JAMIE. No idea. He's quite new. She seems keen.

GEOFF. Are they sleeping together?

JAMIE. She's twenty six, I should hope so. Mind you, quite cautious in that department is our Holly.

GEOFF. Well this is the new age of prudery – didn't you know?

JAMIE. Is it? Glad I missed that.

GEOFF. Yes, well with Diana around you didn't need anyone else, did you?

(DIANA enters.)

Speaking of the devil…

DIANA. Were you talking about me? Nothing nice I hope.

JAMIE. No, horrible. Glad you didn't hear it.

(She kisses GEOFF. Just a casual finger wave to JAMIE.)

DIANA. You're looking apprehensive, Geoff. Are you all right?

GEOFF. Yes, fine.

DIANA. It's us that are getting married, not you.

GEOFF. Yes – speaking of which, Jamie's got something to tell you.

JAMIE. Oh, thanks. I was going to pick my moment.

GEOFF. Better sooner than later.

DIANA. What is it? More complications?

JAMIE. Sort of. Father's got another thirty people to add to the list. Highly important business people apparently.

DIANA. Oh heavens, this thing's becoming just a showcase.

JAMIE. Well at least he's splitting the costs with your side. Will the hotel be able to fit them in?

DIANA. Oh yes. That vast room needs filling up anyway. *(brightly)* Perhaps there'll be so many there no-one will notice if we're not.

JAMIE. Yes! We could do the church service and then skip off. Somewhere nobody could find us, like Blackpool.

GEOFF. The enthusiasm for this wedding is overwhelming.

DIANA. Well let's face it, Geoff, we have been together a long time. We're like an old married couple already.

GEOFF. *(with feeling)* Yes, you are.

DIANA. Which is good. Tried and tested. No unpleasant surprises.

JAMIE. Oh, I've a few up my sleeve yet.

DIANA. Oh goody. I look forward to that.

(ANN *enters from the garden with a bowl. Pulls off gardening gloves.*)

ANN. Hello, lovely people. What's this – a committee meeting?

GEOFF. It's a reception committee.

ANN. Not the wedding reception! Please don't start changing things – I've got it all planned!

JAMIE. No, Mother, don't panic. Reception as in welcome.

ANN. Oh, for Holly and her new boyfriend. Yes – when are they due?

JAMIE. They're here already.

ANN. Already? Have I missed them? Where are they?

GEOFF. She's showing him his room.

ANN. Oh, I should be doing that! How awful – I wasn't here to greet him.

JAMIE. He's fine, Mother. He's had quite enough of us to face for the moment.

ANN. What's he like, Diana?

DIANA. I haven't met him yet.

ANN. Jamie?

JAMIE. Oh, I think he'll just about scrape through the entrance exam.

ANN. *(to* GEOFF*)* Good looking?

GEOFF. *(so-so gesture)* Mmm.

ANN. Dressed properly?

JAMIE. If you like rap, hippy, dropout sort of thing.

ANN. No!

DIANA. Boys, stop it. If I know Holly, he'll be very nice, Ann.

ANN. Oh, I do hope so. It's high time she found someone decent.

DIANA. The others were hardly indecent.

ANN. You know what I mean. Someone *permanent.*

JAMIE. Mother, you've already got one wedding to worry about – you don't need another just yet.

ANN. I know, I know. But my astrologist says the stars are good for this man.

JAMIE. That's practically a guarantee he'll be a washout.

ANN. And they're also excellent for the wedding.

JAMIE. Oh dear.

ANN. Such a cynic, Jamie. I must go up and say hello.

(*goes towards the door, then stops*)

By the way, Diana, your mother asked me over tomorrow to see you having the dress fitted, is that all right?

DIANA. Of course, Ann.

ANN. It won't be breaking protocol or anything?

DIANA. I don't think people worry too much about protocol these days.

ANN. Oh, good. I'm dying to see it. *(hesitates again)* Oh, and Jamie – all these extra banker friends of your father's. We must look at the plans and suggest whereabouts on the tables to put them.

JAMIE. How about underneath?

ANN. *(sighing)* I know it's a bore, but you especially should be glad of a few more influential people to meet.

JAMIE. True, Mother. As the most unpopular species on the planet, the least we can do is all stick together.

ANN. *Such* a cynic, my darling. *(a frisson of pleasure)* Less than four weeks to go – I can't wait! *(holds up the bowl)* Raspberries for supper!

(goes)

JAMIE. Well, it's worth it just to see her so happy. *(follows her to the door)* I'd better get to those plans before she does, and wrecks all that work we've done so far. Do you two want to come?

GEOFF. No thanks.

DIANA. Lord no! Any more discussion on who can't sit with who and I'll want to shoot myself.

(JAMIE goes.)

GOEFF. I thought my suggestion was best. Put all the names in a hat and let everyone take pot luck.

DIANA. Absolutely. Far more interesting. Can you see Ann going along with that?

GEOFF. No.

DIANA. Why is it that every wedding I know has always driven everyone to distraction?

GEOFF. Good preparation for actual marriage probably.

DIANA. Mm.

GEOFF. Diana.

DIANA. Mm?

GEOFF. I've been wanting to get you on your own for weeks.

DIANA. What is it?

GEOFF. You can't marry Jamie.

(pause)

DIANA. What?

GEOFF. You just can't do it.

DIANA. Why, is he married already?

GEOFF. Because it's mad.

DIANA. Mad??

GEOFF. Deep down you know it's mad.

DIANA. *(stunned)* What are you talking about??

GEOFF. He's just not the one for you.

DIANA. Not the…! We've been together for years! We've been together all our lives practically.

GEOFF. I know. That's the point.

DIANA. What are you saying, Geoff?

GEOFF. You've just drifted into this situation. Because… because you've known nothing else. Because the whole world assumed that was what would happen – from the start. But you've never really thought about it – either of you.

DIANA. Of course we've thought about it! We've thought of nothing else for the last year!

GEOFF. You've thought of nothing but the *ceremony* for the last year. Thanks to Jamie's mother, and to your parents, and to…I don't know – to convention. You've never really thought about being *married.*

DIANA. But we are married, Geoff. We've been more or less living together for the last four years.

GEOFF. Exactly. You said it yourself, you're like an old married couple on their golden wedding anniversary. Who've settled for each other because nothing better came along.

DIANA. Oh my God, Geoff…! I can't believe I'm hearing this.

GEOFF. You eat the same cereals for breakfast, you share the same toothpaste, you even wear the same pyjamas for Christ's sake!

DIANA. They're jolly nice pyjamas!

GEOFF. You're both treating marriage as something that just happens, like catching flu! But it's the rest of your life, Di.

DIANA. Well of course...

GEOFF. You'll settle down, you'll do up your house, you'll have your kids – and then one day, not too far off, you'll wake up and think, 'Bloody hell, I'm bored out of my mind!'

(She stares at him.)

You're half bored out of your mind now.

DIANA. *(bewildered)* What...? I don't...What is it you're saying?

GEOFF. I'm saying your life is worth more than that. I'm saying this is your last chance. Jamie's great. Jamie's my best friend...but that's why I know you can't marry him.

DIANA. Why not?

GEOFF. Because he's...not big enough.

DIANA. Big enough? What...what does that mean?

GEOFF. You know what it means.

DIANA. Are you talking about his mind or his willy?

GEOFF. Don't be facetious.

DIANA. And who is big enough?

GEOFF. I am.

(long pause)

DIANA. You?

GEOFF. Yes.

DIANA. I've known you almost as long as Jamie.

GEOFF. Exactly. That's why you know I'm big enough. And I'm not talking about my willy.

DIANA. You…We…We'd fight like cat and dog.

GEOFF. Yeh. We'd challenge each other.

DIANA. Our lives would be like a big dipper ride.

GEOFF. Better than a pedal boat on the village pond.

DIANA. *(at a loss)* I…I…

GEOFF. Di, I've wanted you all my life. I just haven't had the guts to tell you. And we're so right. Think about it. Who do you come to to discuss your problems? Me. Who do you turn to organise the expeditions, the parties, the hangover cures? Me. Who do you talk with about ambitions? Me.

DIANA. Jamie and I have ambitions.

GEOFF. Yes. Ambitions of turning into your parents.

DIANA. No!

GEOFF. Swanky home. Holidays in posh hotels. Social lives avoiding anyone who hasn't got at least a CBE and a couple of Bentleys to rub together. Do you really want to end up like his folks?

DIANA. We don't…we needn't…

GEOFF. And there's another thing.

DIANA. What?

GEOFF. Sex.

DIANA. What about it?

GEOFF. You never have sex with Jamie like you had with me.

DIANA. How do you know? How do you…?

GEOFF. Be honest. You have never had bonking with Jamie even remotely competing with what you and I had that weekend in Yorkshire.

DIANA. *(glancing nervously at the door)* That was a freak weekend. That was a one-off. That should never have happened.

GEOFF. It did happen, Di. And it was the best sex of your life. Admit it. It was certainly the best sex of my life. Every other woman I've had since, I've had to pretend was you.

DIANA. Oh God, Geoff…

GEOFF. Do you have orgasms like that with Jamie?

DIANA. This is embarrassing!

GEOFF. This is crucial.

DIANA. All right, so I came with you – that's…

GEOFF. Four or five times if I remember.

DIANA. Multiple orgasms don't make a marriage, Geoff!

GEOFF. They're an indication of what the marriage could be like. Excitement, challenge, joy!

DIANA. You can have too much of that as well. Big dippers can be just as risky as pedal boats.

GEOFF. Yes, but at least one has tried. At least one has flown high. At least one has gone for it!

(Pause. She stares at him.)

Be honest, Diana. You must have thought about it yourself – occasionally.

DIANA. Occasionally, but I…I never…I mean, it's impossible. There's a monster wedding planned in four weeks time. There are guests and presents and… How could we face all our parents?

GEOFF. We just say the roles have changed. You tell them you're marrying me instead.

DIANA. It's insane! Can you see my parents? 'Oh really darling? – dear old Geoff, that's nice. Just so long as he wears clean underwear and doesn't snore.'

GEOFF. Di…

DIANA. It's not possible! You have to have banns read. You have to…

GEOFF. At least you're thinking about it.

DIANA. No, I'm not! It's *un*thinkable.

GEOFF. We just make it a blessing, a service of betrothal. Everything else stays the same.

DIANA. What about Jamie? How could I explain to Jamie?

GEOFF. I'll do that. I'll break it to him first. Then if he kills me it'll solve everyone's problems.

DIANA. Oh sure!

GEOFF. My feeling is he'll be as relieved as you are.

DIANA. I'm not relieved, Geoff! I'm appalled! I'm distraught! My whole world has turned on its head!

GEOFF. Good. It needed to.

DIANA. Not like this! Not one month before my wedding!

GEOFF. *(coming to her)* Kiss me.

DIANA. *(breaking away)* That's the last thing I'm going to do! Look, Geoff, all right I agree we're good together...

GEOFF. Yes.

DIANA. ...I agree the sex was great...

GEOFF. Yes!

DIANA. ...I agree with most of what you say.

GEOFF. So?

DIANA. But how do we know that our relationship would be any more successful than mine and Jamie's?

GEOFF. We don't. Relationships have to be worked at.

DIANA. Well...

GEOFF. We've all been around enough to know you don't just walk into a crowded room and see a stranger and wham, bang – that's it for ever. That's an adolescent fantasy.

DIANA. Perhaps it is, but...

GEOFF. Do you still believe in it?

DIANA. Of course not!

GEOFF. Well then. What do you say? It's now or never, Di. It's the whole of the rest of your life.

DIANA. Don't say things like that!

GEOFF. And if I wasn't certain you weren't certain yourself, and that Jamie was even less certain, then I wouldn't be as certain as I am about saying what I'm saying.

DIANA. That's gobbledygook!

GEOFF. Maybe but you know what it means. Well then?

DIANA. I need time.

GEOFF. You haven't got much. The longer you take, the harder it's going to be. But I'll give you this weekend.

DIANA. Is that an ultimatum?

GEOFF. Yes.

DIANA. And if I can't decide.

GEOFF. I'll announce it for you.

DIANA. Oh God...

(sounds from the hall)

GEOFF. Someone's coming. I'll leave you to think about it.

*(He nips hurriedly out of the garden door. **DIANA** sits in a daze. Then bursts into floods of tears. **HOLLY** enters.)*

HOLLY. Well that's the first hurdle over. Tom is charming the pants off Mother, and... *(notices **DIANA**)* Di? What is it, Di? *(runs to her and holds her)* Oh, my love, what is it?

*(**DIANA** buries her head in **HOLLY**'s shoulder weeping.)*

DIANA. Oh God, Holly, what am I going to do?

HOLLY. What is it? What's happened?

DIANA. *(gasping)* I...I don't...I can't...

HOLLY. Take deep breaths. Tell me. What is it?

DIANA. It's Geoff. He says I can't marry Jamie. I should be marrying him.

HOLLY. Geoff?

DIANA. He says he's much righter for me than Jamie is. He says Jamie and me are...are like a boring old pair of pensioners!

HOLLY. Well you are a bit.

*(more wails from **DIANA**)*

But I mean...well that's good. You match each other, like old socks.

(more wails)

But what...? I mean why does he say you should be marrying him?

DIANA. He says he's always wanted me. He says we complement each other. He says with him life would be challenging...

HOLLY. Well that's true.

DIANA. He says…he says…Oh God, I've forgotten all he said now, but it sort of made sense.

HOLLY. Do you fancy him?

DIANA. That's the trouble. You mustn't tell Jamie this, but a year or two ago Geoff and I had a weekend fling. It just came on us out of the blue. And it was wonderful.

HOLLY. Oh dear…This is serious.

DIANA. Do you think he's right?

HOLLY. Um…could be.

DIANA. But how can we possibly? How could we tell everyone?

HOLLY. Um…

DIANA. He says the arrangements could just stay virtually the same, but with him instead of Jamie.

HOLLY. That's true.

DIANA. But how could I tell Jamie?

HOLLY. Um…

DIANA. He says Jamie's as bored with our relationship as I am.

HOLLY. That's true.

DIANA. But how could we tell all the parents? How could we tell your mother?

HOLLY. Um…

DIANA. He says marrying the right person is more important than saving her wedding plans.

HOLLY. That's true.

DIANA. But how can we be sure we'd be any better together than me and Jamie?

HOLLY. Um…

DIANA. He says there's no such thing as perfect love at first sight – it has to be worked at.

HOLLY. That's true.

DIANA. Will you stop saying that's true! You're not helping!

HOLLY. Well, much as I love my brother, I have to say, looking back, you and Geoff were always better suited to each other.

DIANA. Oh hell.

HOLLY. And Jamie would get over it. He gets over everything, one way or another.

DIANA. Oh God.

HOLLY. And Mother would eventually get over it too, just as long as she still had her party arrangements in place.

DIANA. Oh hell.

HOLLY. And even though it would now be Geoff's parents hosting it with yours, the guest list would stay much the same, except that Father would have to cancel his new business invitations, which would leave thirty places free for their special people.

DIANA. Oh God.

HOLLY. And his folks would be quite pleased because they've always secretly fancied you as Geoff's other half.

DIANA. Oh hell.

HOLLY. So one way and another…Let's ask *The Thinker*. *(goes to the statuette and stares at it for a second)* Yep – says it's a viable proposition.

DIANA. Oh Holly…Lord, what a maelstrom your new man's walked into! I haven't met him yet. He'll run a mile when he sees what's happening here.

HOLLY. No, he'll be quite intrigued probably. He's certainly never met a species like us.

DIANA. Was it love at first sight with him?

HOLLY. God, no. I thought he was dishy. But I had no idea how it would work. Still don't.

DIANA. Is sex good?

HOLLY. We've only done it a couple of times. Haven't really got into the swing yet.

DIANA. Well don't let it just drift on, that's all I can say. Oh, what am I going to do?

HOLLY. Do you really agree with all that Geoff said?

DIANA. Sort of. Most of it.

HOLLY. Then you have no choice. Take a deep breath and go for it, Di. He's a lucky man. Isn't he, Thinker?

(Nods for the statuette. Voices from the hall.)

Here they come. Shall we tell them?

DIANA. No! No. Let me think. I'll do it when I'm ready.

(ANN and JAMIE enter.)

ANN. Well, he's very nice your young man, Holly dear. Makes a good job of flattering prospective mothers-in-law.

HOLLY. We're a very long way from that, Mother. Don't you dare start speculating. Where is he?

ANN. He took one look at the new multi-jet shower in the guest bathroom and said he had to try it. So I left him to it.

HOLLY. Good. Out of harm's way for a bit.

ANN. What's going on here? Diana? Are you all right?

DIANA. *(covering up)* Yes, yes. Just a bit emotional.

ANN. It's always an emotional time, dear. But make the most of it. You'll long for a bit of emotion later on.

JAMIE. Great, Mother, that's a big help.

ANN. Well comfort her, Jamie. She's your responsibility.

JAMIE. *(going to DIANA)* Are you O.K. old thing? Can I help?

DIANA. No, Jamie, I'm all right. *(turns to him)* Jamie, you do want this wedding, don't you?

JAMIE. 'Course I do. We're not going through all this bloody palaver unless we want it, are we?

DIANA. No.

JAMIE. Why d'you ask?

DIANA. I wanted to know your true feelings.

JAMIE. Everyone has doubts just before the big day, Di. It's natural.

DIANA. Do they?

JAMIE. Don't they, Mother?

ANN. Oh yes. I've had them ever since.

HOLLY. Mother!

ANN. Sorry. Don't worry, Diana. Marriage is a splendid institution. We'd all be much worse off out of it than in it.

JAMIE. Well that's a terrific recommendation – thanks very much, Mother.

ANN. I can see I'm not helping. I'll go and see if...there's enough potatoes for dinner.

(Goes. Pause. **JAMIE** *looks from* **DIANA** *to* **HOLLY***.)*

HOLLY. Well...the coast's clear. Now's as good a time as ever.

DIANA. No! Don't you say a word!

JAMIE. What is it? Am I missing something?

DIANA. No, Jamie. I just need a little time to think about things, that's all.

JAMIE. What things?

DIANA. Just things in general.

HOLLY. Well, er...I think I'd better slide off and leave you two alone.

DIANA. No, Holly! Don't leave us!

HOLLY. Well, I'm not really...I mean, I can't I couldn't...I need the bathroom.

DIANA. *(calling after her)* Come straight back.

*(***HOLLY*** goes. Awkward pause.)*

JAMIE. What's going on?

DIANA. Um...Tell me, Jamie, are you...

JAMIE. Am I what?

DIANA. Truly happy about marrying me?

JAMIE. Well, Keira Knightley said no, so...

DIANA. Be serious!

JAMIE. Well of course I am.

DIANA. Truly?

JAMIE. Of course I…Aren't you happy?

DIANA. I was just wondering whether you were serious about the wedding, or just going along with it because everyone else was.

JAMIE. Going along with it?

DIANA. Yes.

JAMIE. I…that's…It would cause one hell of a shemozzle to pull out after all the agony that's gone into it.

DIANA. But surely you'd rather endure the shemozzle than a lifetime of the wrong marriage.

JAMIE. I'm not sure – I'd have to think about that one.

DIANA. I'm serious, Jamie.

JAMIE. Are you saying…are you telling me you've decided it's the wrong marriage?

DIANA. No. I'm just asking you for *your* opinion.

JAMIE. We've been together for four years, Di. You don't do that if it's wrong.

DIANA. Yes, but don't you feel we may be a bit…stuck in a rut?

JAMIE. I'd rather be stuck in a rut than alone in the ditch.

DIANA. Thanks, that's a great reassurance.

JAMIE. *(taking her hands)* It's just prenuptial nerves, sweetheart. It's just the prospect of this bloody great shindig. Once it's over you and I can settle down and organise our own private hassle-free existence without having to worry about everyone else.

DIANA. Yes.

JAMIE. Done and dusted. Settled for life. Think what a relief it'll be.

(She stares into space. It is the nail in the coffin.)

DIANA. Yes.

JAMIE. You don't seem very sure.

DIANA. You're only thirty, Jamie. I'm twenty seven. I'm not certain I'm ready to be done and dusted. Sounds like an old settee.

JAMIE. Have you...?

DIANA. What?

JAMIE. Met someone else?

DIANA. Someone else?

JAMIE. Someone new.

DIANA. No.

JAMIE. Well that's a relief.

(a beat)

DIANA. What if you did?

JAMIE. What do you mean?

DIANA. What would you do? If you met a Keira Knightley lookalike – after we were married?

JAMIE. Ah, well...

DIANA. Watch it!

JAMIE. Look, Di. We're not kids. We've both sowed our wild oats. There's no point at this stage worrying about the future. For God's sake, what's got into you?

DIANA. Sorry. I'm not quite myself today.

JAMIE. For what it's worth, Di, you're the best girl, the most beautiful, the most level-headed, the biggest catch around – apart from Keira Knightley. Everyone thinks so. And therefore I'm the luckiest guy around to be able to call you mine. I'm not giving that up so easily.

DIANA. I see. I'm a trophy wife.

JAMIE. No! That's not what I...That's not it.

DIANA. Then what is it?

JAMIE. It's...it's I've always thought of you as mine. I can't change that thought now – just because everyone's a but uptight about the wedding.

DIANA. Shouldn't we be thrilled about the wedding?

JAMIE. Well...yes, but...I mean...

DIANA. Perhaps we're uptight because deep down we're not sure about it. Perhaps we're just doing it because he says it's logical. *(indicates* The Thinker*)*

(He stares at her.)

JAMIE. So we should only do it if it's illogical?

DIANA. No, that's not...I didn't mean...*(gasps with frustration)* Oh!

*(**HOLLY** sticks her head back in.)*

HOLLY. Everything all right? Do you want me back in?

DIANA. Yes, Holly. Come in.

HOLLY. *(doing so)* Are you, er...? Have you...? Would you like me to do anything?

DIANA. Yes. You could get everyone back in here. I've something to discuss with them all.

HOLLY. *(wide-eyed)* Right. I'll do that.

(She hurries back out.)

JAMIE. What? What are you going to discuss?

DIANA. Just wait a moment, Jamie. Let's wait till they're all here.

JAMIE. I don't like this at all. Why can't you tell me now?

HOLLY. *(off)* Mother! Geoff!

DIANA. I've only the strength to do this once, Jamie. I think I need to say it to everyone at the same time.

JAMIE. You've got me really scared now. What are you going to say?

HOLLY. *(off, calling out to the garden)* Geoff! Can you come inside, please.

DIANA. Don't look at me like that.

JAMIE. How do you expect me to look? Why won't you tell me?

DIANA. Just wait will you, Jamie!

*(He gestures acceptance. She moves away. They wait in silence. **ANN** and **HOLLY** enter from the hall.)*

ANN. What is it? What's happening?

HOLLY. I think Diana wants to tell us something.

*(**GEOFF** comes in from the garden. He says nothing, just looks at **DIANA**.)*

DIANA. Please – sit down everyone.

ANN. *(sitting)* What's going on? Everyone's acting so strangely today.

*(They are all seated in a semi circle. **DIANA** stands in front of them.)*

DIANA. I'm sorry to do this to you all. I know I've caused a bit of a turmoil this morning. Especially to you, Jamie. I just…I have to…There's something I need to…

*(She wanders, hand to forehead, at a loss how to begin. At that moment **TOM** sticks his head round the door.)*

TOM. Hello?

*(all turn, except **DIANA** who has her back to him)*

HOLLY. Oh, Tom!

TOM. Sorry, is this not a good moment?

HOLLY. *(rising, uncertain)* Er…come in…er…we were just… it's a little family discussion…but please, um…

TOM. Oh, then I won't intrude. I'll er….

*(sees **DIANA**'s back)*

Oh. Is this…? Is this the bride?

HOLLY. Of course, you haven't met! Um…Diana, this is Tom. Tom, Diana.

*(**DIANA** turns. She and **TOM** face each other with **HOLLY** in between them. They stare at each other, struck dumb. **HOLLY** prattles on, too concerned as to how to deal with the situation to notice.)*

It's a bit difficult at the moment, Tom. You see we were just having a little family…a sort of strategy meeting about the wedding, and…well, I don't suppose it matters if you, er…I mean, you'll have to know all about it in any case at some stage. It's just a question of whether Diana wants you, er…*(gives up)* Oh hell, I don't know! Diana, I leave it to you to decide.

DIANA. *(coming out of her daze)* Er…sorry, what…?

HOLLY. Does it matter if Tom stays for this?

DIANA. *(locking eyes with* **TOM** *again)* Tom? No, er...no, he can stay.

HOLLY. Fine. Well you'd better, um...you'd better sit here, Tom.

TOM. *(distracted)* Sorry?

HOLLY. *(indicating)* Take that chair.

TOM. Oh...yes. Sorry.

(Sits to the side, spellbound by **DIANA**. *She pulls herself together, but is now in a state of total shock.)*

ANN. Carry on then, darling.

DIANA. I...What was I saying?

JAMIE. You were about to tell us something that is apparently very important.

DIANA. Yes. Yes, I was...But I don't think...I don't know how to say it.

JAMIE. Why not? You were dead set on it just now.

DIANA. I've lost the, er...I don't think I can say it now after all. I...

(She sits. **GEOFF** *rises.)*

GEOFF. Very well. Then I'll say it.

ANN. You, Geoff? How do you know what she wants to say?

GEOFF. Because it involves me, Ann.

(He takes centre floor. **DIANA** *and* **TOM** *are facing each other from different sides of the room. Throughout the following they simply stare at each other.)*

I'm desperately sorry about this, Jamie. And you Ann. And you Tom – you've walked into a whirlwind. But I had to do it. Earlier on I told Diana that she shouldn't be marrying Jamie. She should be marrying me.

(gasps, then stunned silence)

I told her that the only reason she and Jamie were marrying was because they'd got stuck in a rut and they had nowhere else to go. I told her she was settling for the status quo because that's what was expected of her, but that it could only lead to indifference and stalemate and ultimate tedium.

JAMIE. Thanks.

GEOFF. No reflection, Jamie – it's just the way your relationship is. I told her that life with me, though risky no doubt, would be far more exciting and ambitious and challenging because...well because that's the way *we* are. I told her that I've always felt this way about her, and that I had to do something about it now before it was too late.

(pause)

There. I've said it. And I'm pretty sure Diana agrees with me.

ANN. Oh my goodness!

GEOFF. Yes, I know, Ann – this seems like a cataclysm after all your preparations for the wedding. But it needn't be. We can keep the arrangements, we can turn it into a service of betrothal, we can stick with more or less the same guest list, my parents I'm sure will be happy to take over their share of the costs, and if they don't I'll sell everything I have and pay for it myself.

ANN. Oh my heavens!

GEOFF. What Jamie is going to say, or Diana's parents, or your husband, Ann, for that matter, I've no idea. But if it's horse whips, shotguns, and pistols at dawn – well so be it.

ANN. Oh my lord!

GEOFF. Diana?

(She tears her eyes away from **TOM** *and looks at him.)*

DIANA. *(small voice)* Yes?

GEOFF. Have you anything to say?

DIANA. Me?

GEOFF. Yes.

DIANA. No.

GEOFF. Nothing to add?

DIANA. No.

GEOFF. Jamie?

JAMIE. *(dazed)* No.

GEOFF. I've no doubt you will later. Well then – that's it. There we are.

ANN. Oh Jamie, my poor darling. Had you any idea this was coming?

JAMIE. No.

ANN. How does it make you feel?

JAMIE. Nothing. I don't feel a thing.

ANN. You're in shock.

HOLLY. How do *you* feel, Mum?

ANN. Well I'm in shock too. I never...it hadn't occurred to me. Diana and Geoff. Oh, my heavens! Has there...has there been something between you before this?

(awkward moment)

GEOFF. Well we know each other almost as well as she and Jamie do. I mean it's not exactly a flash in the pan.

ANN. No. But...well, it might have been a slow braise in the pot. It seems so sudden.

GEOFF. Yes, I'm sorry.

ANN. I'll have to have a serious talk with my astrologist!

HOLLY. Yes, Mum, you'd better sack him this time.

ANN. Diana, darling, you're very quiet. Have you nothing to say about it?

DIANA. *(quiet)* Um...I think Geoff has said it all. I'm so sorry everyone.

ANN. So you want us to go ahead with the whole thing – service and reception and everything – with just the names changed? Including Jamie now as best man, I suppose! *(pause)* Is that right?

DIANA. *(in a whisper)* Yes.

ANN. Sorry, I can't hear.

DIANA. *(louder)* Yes.

ANN. Oh my lord! Well, I...Well, if everyone's sure of what they're doing, we'd better...I suppose we must...I don't know if anything like this has ever happened before! Has it?

GEOFF. Um...I think it happened in *High Society*.

ANN. Yes, well she's not Grace Kelly and you're certainly not Bing Crosby. I mean, there'll be mayhem! You'll all have to explain to your various parents. I'll have to telephone Father, if I can find him wherever he is in Europe. There's all our friends. It'll be a holocaust! The airways will be clogged for days!

(She rises.)

Right – Jamie, Holly, come with me. We need a family conference about how to handle this. You'd better bring the bloody Thinker with you! Diana, you must...

(sees DIANA sitting frozen)

No, Diana, you'd better just stay there for the moment. Will you excuse us everyone. Oh my heavens!

(Sweeps from the room. JAMIE and HOLLY follow, the latter giving DIANA thumbs up as she leaves.)

(Pause. DIANA and TOM still sit immobile. GEOFF fidgets awkwardly.)

GEOFF. Well – we did it. *(pause)* Bit of a shock for you to walk into, Tom.

TOM. Yes.

GEOFF. *(to DIANA)* Are you all right, Di?

DIANA. Yes.

GEOFF. Went better than I expected. At least there weren't heart attacks and hysterics and fisticuffs all round the furniture. Do you...? Would you like to come home with me and explain to my parents?

DIANA. No. Not just now.

GEOFF. Shall I come with you and explain to *your* parents?

DIANA. Not just now.

GEOFF. Right. Well, I suppose they can wait a little... Perhaps I'd better leave and let the dust settle. I'll see you later this evening...when you've had time to recover. Then we can talk things over more calmly. *(pause)* Is that a good idea?

DIANA. Yes, Geoff. You go home now.

GEOFF. Right...yes...OK...

(He hesitates, smiles awkwardly at **TOM,** *and leaves. Silence.)*

DIANA. *(eventually)* I...

TOM. No! Don't say anything.

DIANA. Right.

(silence)

TOM. *(eventually)* I don't...I don't know what to do.

DIANA. Me neither.

(pause)

TOM. I've...I've never before...

DIANA. Me neither.

(pause)

TOM. *(rising)* I think I'd better...go and do something.

DIANA. Right.

(He goes. She is alone. Pause.)

Oh God.

(blackout)

SCENE TWO

(Two hours later. **ANN** *wanders up and down speaking on the telephone.)*

ANN. ...I know darling, can you believe it! And we don't know whether to send out new invitations, or simply let everyone turn up and find out what's happened on the day. Wouldn't that cause a sensation! ...I know, can you believe it! But then of course there's all the presents they've chosen. They might not want to spend as much if they know she's marrying somebody else. And the vicar nearly passed out on the end of the phone. He says he's done betrothal services but not in front of two hundred people, with the betrothed in a wedding dress. He said he ought to change his address to the Sermon on the Mount...Yes, can you believe it! And you can imagine my husband's reaction. He has to let half the City know they're not invited after all. He says it might just cause a stock market crash...I know, can you believe it! I'm thinking of firing my astrologist. All right, sweetheart, I'll keep you posted...I know, I can't believe it!

(shuts down the phone, just as **GEOFF** *enters diffidently)*

GEOFF. Oh, Ann...hello, I'm back.

ANN. Well, Geoff!

GEOFF. I know. I just felt I had to see Jamie again to try and put things right. Well, I know I can't do that, but perhaps explain a bit better. Well I know I can't do that, but perhaps...well I don't know what I can do, but...

ANN. Well whatever you do, I think you'll find him in the study.

GEOFF. Is he all right?

ANN. Seems quite resigned actually. Diana's still here too somewhere.

GEOFF. Diana?

ANN. She said she can't face her parents just yet. I must say she's in a strangely subdued mood for someone who's just discovered their true love. Ha – True Love! High Society again. Have you been singing Bing Crosby songs to her?

GEOFF. No.

ANN. Well something must have turned her head. Have you told your parents?

GEOFF. Yes.

ANN. How did they react?

GEOFF. Father said, 'How much is it going to cost me?', and Mother said, 'About time too, I thought you'd never get round to it.'

ANN. It seems everyone could see it coming except us. I must say, you've hit us with a bombshell.

GEOFF. I'm so sorry. I left it far too late, but I…I just never had the courage or the opportunity before.

ANN. It's strange – I can't adjust to the idea of being a guest now at what I thought was my wedding.

GEOFF. You've put so much work into it. Diana and I will always be grateful.

ANN. Well I suppose so. But do you really think you should go ahead with everything before you've had a chance to really think about it?

GEOFF. I've thought about it for ever. And as everything's organised…it would be such a waste to abandon it all now.

ANN. *(with a sigh)* Well all I can say, Geoff, is if someone had to take her away from us I'm glad it was you.

GEOFF. That's very generous of you.

ANN. Now we just have to start all over again finding someone new for Jamie. I only hope we've got Holly sorted – at least it would be one less to worry about.

GEOFF. You don't have to worry about either of them – they're both highly attractive people.

ANN. That's no guarantee of anything. And just wait until you're a parent – worrying is part of the contract.

(**HOLLY** *enters.*)

HOLLY. Oh Geoff, you're back. Wow, isn't this dramatic?

ANN. I don't know why you're so excited about it all. I gather you were part of the conspiracy.

HOLLY. Don't blame me. I was just a shoulder for Diana to cry on.

ANN. Why was she crying if it's all such a wonderful outcome?

HOLLY. Oh Mother, stop being so dismal about it. It's the best thing for everyone. Now where's Tom? Has anyone seen him? He seems to have hidden away somewhere.

ANN. I'm not surprised. I should think he's fled in terror from the prospect of joining such a mad family.

HOLLY. He's not so cowardly, and that prospect hasn't remotely arisen yet. I hardly know him.

ANN. You've been to bed with him, haven't you?

HOLLY. Mother!!

ANN. Well everyone seems to do that these days before they've even shaken hands. Anyway just remember, if you're going to sneak into his room tonight at least do it after everyone else is asleep.

HOLLY. Well if that's the rule why didn't you put us in the same room to start with?

ANN. Don't be ridiculous, darling – everyone knows what's happening, but everyone has to pretend they don't. It's called etiquette. He'd be the first to be embarrassed if we didn't.

GEOFF. That's true.

ANN. And talking of etiquette, I must send those table plans over to your parents, Geoff. At least that headache is theirs now.

GEOFF. Oh Christ, what have I done?

ANN. Saved me a lot of work for one thing.

HOLLY. And saved two people from a fate worse than death.

ANN. That's a bit strong, dear.

GEOFF. How do we know? How does anyone know? They might have been very happy being placid together. And we might end up trying to kill each other – look at half the marriages around you.

ANN. Quite.

HOLLY. Yes, well that's a highly constructive attitude to start off with. *(hugs him)* I think you'll be terrific together.

GEOFF. Can I live up to her, that's the thing?

ANN. Probably not, but there's no harm in trying.

HOLLY. Mother! You're not helping.

ANN. Sorry.

HOLLY. *(going to the window)* now where has that man of mine got to? It's quite strange. He vanished after the great revelation and I haven't seen him since.

ANN. Well, as I said, he might have run for cover.

GEOFF. If he has he's too much of a wimp for Holly.

HOLLY. He's not a wimp. But he may be susceptible to culture shocks.

(**JAMIE** *enters.*)

JAMIE. Ah. I'm surprised you've dared to come back.

GEOFF. Jamie, I just felt I ought to…

JAMIE. Don't. I'd rather you didn't. I've been thinking these past couple of hours. I've decided I'm going to write off this period of my life as an aberration. Start again with a completely new persona.

HOLLY. That's a great plan.

ANN. What's the persona going to be, dear?

JAMIE. Dunno quite yet. Might become a wildly promiscuous druggy. Might go into the church. Might go to India and sit on a mountain top.

GEOFF. Bit of a waste that. Why not combine the other two. Promiscuous clergyman – I can see you as that.

JAMIE. Yeh, that sounds good. Then I could marry off people like you and Diana – after first seducing the bride of course.

ANN. No need to be irreverent, Jamie.

JAMIE. Did you by the way?

GEOFF. What?

JAMIE. Seduce her?

GEOFF. Diana?

JAMIE. Yes.

GEOFF. What makes you think that?

JAMIE. There has to be more to this than just a meeting of minds. So?

(embarrassed moment)

ANN. *(awkward)* I think I'd better go and...

JAMIE. No, Mother, stay. You should know the facts like the rest of us.

HOLLY. Jamie, I don't think...

JAMIE. Quiet, you. Well?

GEOFF. Once. A long time ago.

ANN. Oh dear.

JAMIE. *(puzzled)* A long time ago?

GEOFF. Two years.

JAMIE. Two years? You both had it off two years ago and you've only just decided now that you fancy each other?

GEOFF. We've always fancied each other. We just...

JAMIE. What?

GEOFF. Couldn't do anything while she was with you.

JAMIE. *(frowning)* I don't quite understand that. You and she were so attracted to each other two years ago that you couldn't help leaping into bed together, and yet... Was it good by the way?

ANN. Jamie...!

JAMIE. Was it?

GEOFF. Yes.

JAMIE. *(nodding)* And yet you then wait all that time before deciding you needed to do it again…regularly on an official basis.

HOLLY. Jamie…

JAMIE. Quiet, you.

GEOFF. I decided long ago. I just didn't know how Diana felt. And I didn't want to…

JAMIE. What?

GEOFF. Get in between you.

JAMIE. I see. So you wait until we're actually getting married before you get in between us?

GEOFF. Yeh. Cowardly, wasn't it?

JAMIE. Bloody heroic, I'd say. Tell me, where did this explosive sexual union take place? Her bedroom?

ANN. *(eyes closed)* Ohh!

GEOFF. No, in Yorkshire. That time she wanted to go up and trace her family history.

JAMIE. Oh yes, I remember. And you had a convention or something near there at the same time.

GEOFF. Yes.

JAMIE. Good lord! I even suggested you took her up instead of me because I didn't fancy trekking round freezing windswept graveyards.

GEOFF. Yes.

JAMIE. What a fool I was. Never occurred to me I might be setting you up for a free shag.

ANN. *(eyes to heaven)* Where did I go wrong with this family?

GEOFF. It wasn't like that. It just hit us out of the blue.

JAMIE. Oh, I see. 'Oh look, there's Auntie Betty's grave. Looks nice and grassy – let's have a quick one on it.'

GEOFF. Jamie, please…

JAMIE. No, I'm interested. How did it happen?

HOLLY. Jamie!

JAMIE. Quiet, you.

HOLLY. Bully!

GEOFF. We just had dinner at the hotel – pretty awful one if I remember – a bit too much wine of course…and we talked and talked.

JAMIE. And one thing led to another.

GEOFF. No, not really. We went up together with no thought of…well, I always had the thought if I'm honest…

JAMIE. Aha!

GEOFF. But I had no intention of…anyway we got to our separate rooms and said goodnight…and then she tripped over a frayed bit of carpet in hers and twisted her ankle. It was quite painful and I was putting a cold compress on it, and…well, it just happened.

JAMIE. I see. 'Thank you, doctor. A good seeing to – just the cure I needed.' Have I grounds for suing the hotel for negligently wrecking my marriage, do you think?

ANN. I can't take any more of this. I'm going to find something to do in the kitchen.

(goes out)

HOLLY. *(to* **JAMIE***)* This is awful. If this is your new persona, I don't like it.

JAMIE. Oh sorry. As a clergyman I must remember, a principle of the faith is forgiveness.

GEOFF. I don't expect you to forgive, Jamie. I wouldn't if I was in your place.

JAMIE. No. Well I do forgive as a matter of fact. I just need to retaliate a bit to salve my wounded pride.

*(***DIANA*** enters, subdued.)*

DIANA. Hello everyone. Ann said you were all here.

JAMIE. There she is! How's the ankle?

DIANA. Sorry?

JAMIE. The twisted ankle. Healed pretty well, I gather. Unconventional treatment, but hey – whatever works.

DIANA. *(looking at* **GEOFF***)* What…?

GEOFF. Sorry. I had to tell him.

JAMIE. And to think it was me who suggested he went with you to Yorkshire. Little did I know I was sabotaging my own future wedding.

DIANA. I'm sorry, Jamie.

JAMIE. Were there any others? On your trips around the home counties? Or your various visits to medical establishments? Oh doctor, I've got a bit of a frozen relationship here, could you take a look at it for me? Well?

DIANA. No.

JAMIE. *(to* GEOFF*)* And was that the only time between you two?

GEOFF. Yes.

JAMIE. I still don't understand. You had this earth moving experience and yet you wait another two years before deciding you want some more of it.

GEOFF. I've told you, I always wanted it. I just wasn't sure of Diana.

JAMIE. *(to* DIANA*)* So did you always want it? While doing it with me?

DIANA. Perhaps I did – subconsciously

JAMIE. *(nodding thoughtfully)* So I was a subconscious, sublimated surrogate. That's a nice alliterated role, I must say.

DIANA. Jamie…

JAMIE. No, no. It's all right. If I'm brutally honest – and it seems the time for brutal honesty – I have to admit sex was always a touch uninspired between you and me.

(She says nothing.)

Well…I suppose all that's left is to wish you a long and happy union, Diana. May all your graves be soft and all your carpets smooth.

*(***TOM*** enters from the hall.)*

HOLLY. Tom! There you are! Where on earth have you been?

(**DIANA** *immediately turns her back on* **TOM**. *After one quick glance he avoids looking at her.*)

TOM. I, er...I just needed some fresh air. I went for a walk round the village.

HOLLY. Why didn't you tell me? I'd have come with you.

TOM. I sort of wanted to be on my own for a little.

HOLLY. After all the dramatics?

TOM. Yes.

HOLLY. I'm not surprised. You must have wondered what on earth you'd walked into. But don't take it seriously, darling. We aren't this cataclysmic all the time. *(looks at the others)* Mind you, having said that, we're keeping up the tradition quite well at the moment.

TOM. Is this bad timing again?

JAMIE. Don't worry about it, Tom. There's no such thing as good timing round here just now. It's good for you to know what it is you're jumping into...if you are jumping into it...or just skirting round it or perhaps...

HOLLY. Shut up, Jamie!

JAMIE. Right.

TOM. *(making conversation)* Nice little place. Smart houses round here.

GEOFF. Oh yes. Surrounded by Russian oligarchs and Arab magnates and City entrepreneurs here. We're the poor neighbours down this end.

TOM. Mm. Wish I was this poor.

HOLLY. Doesn't make life any easier. Just that your luxuries are now called necessities.

GEOFF. And your indulgences are called essentials.

JAMIE. Like huge weddings.

GEOFF. Exactly.

JAMIE. Which we now know are even more of a farce. Don't we, Di?

(She says nothing.)

Diana?

DIANA. *(turning)* Yes.

JAMIE. You could of course call the whole razzmatazz off. Just have a simple ceremony on the village green or somewhere. Might be the rational thing to do now.

(She and **TOM** *are looking at each other.)*

DIANA. Yes. It might.

GEOFF. Is that what you'd like, Di?

DIANA. *(switching her gaze)* What?

GEOFF. Would you like to call it off?

DIANA. The wedding?

GEOFF. Well…the big showcase wedding. We could make it less of a freak show. The parents would probably be delighted now.

DIANA. Yes.

GEOFF. What do you mean, yes? What sort of a wedding do you want to make it?

DIANA. Er…whatever you wish. Whatever's best.

GEOFF. What's the matter with you, Di? You're behaving very oddly.

DIANA. Am I? Sorry. It's just…the change in circumstances.

GEOFF. Don't tell me you're having second thoughts? After all we've been through.

JAMIE. Third thoughts actually, if you're going to be accurate.

DIANA. No. I…I just can't think very straight at the moment.

*(***ANN*** *enters with a tray of glasses.)*

ANN. Oh, Tom, you've appeared again.

TOM. Yes, sorry.

ANN. That's good, because we need some distraction here. I think it's about drinkies time.

JAMIE. Best suggestion so far.

ANN. Now I was planning to open champagne and have a little celebration for everyone, but perhaps that's not appropriate in the circumstances. Is it?

JAMIE. Oh yes, Mother, by all means let's celebrate. Toast the new era.

ANN. Very well. Jamie, you can come and open bottles for me. And Holly, I'd like some help with the nibbles. We used to call them canapes, Tom, but that's considered pretentious now. We'll leave you three for a moment to, er…get to know each other.

(*Goes.* **JAMIE** *and* **HOLLY** *follow.* **JAMIE** *turns at the door.*)

JAMIE. Please don't plan any more revelations in our absence.

(*Goes. Awkward silence.*)

GEOFF. Well, er…

TOM. Perhaps I ought to go and leave you two…

DIANA. No, Tom, don't go.

GEOFF. Um…don't you think you ought to go and tell your parents, Di? I mean, they're the only ones still in the dark.

DIANA. I don't know how I'm going to explain to them.

GEOFF. Just tell them. You can't beat about the bush. Perhaps…perhaps they may not be as surprised as you think.

DIANA. Oh, I think they will.

(*He shrugs.*)

GEOFF…

GEOFF. What?

DIANA. Would you like to explain to them?

GEOFF. Me?

DIANA. I don't think I could handle them just at the moment. And you'd do it rather better than I would.

GEOFF. Well…if you really want me to…

DIANA. Yes, I would actually. Get it over with. Then I can face them when they've had a little time to digest it.

GEOFF. Well all right. I'll, er…

DIANA. The sooner the better really.

GEOFF. I'll pop round there now then, shall I?

DIANA. No time like the present.

GEOFF. Right.

DIANA. Thank you.

GEOFF. If I'm not back within the hour, you'll know either your mother's been taken off with a heart attack, or your father's shot me.

DIANA. They'll be fine.

(**GEOFF** *goes out by the garden door. The two look at each other. Long silence.*)

TOM. *(eventually)* What are you thinking?

DIANA. You know what I'm thinking.

TOM. The same thing I'm thinking?

DIANA. I think so.

TOM. So...if you *are* thinking what I'm thinking...the next thing I'm thinking...is what on earth are we going to do?

DIANA. Yes.

TOM. So what *are* we going to do?

DIANA. I haven't the faintest idea. *Romeo and Juliet,* I should think.

TOM. What?

DIANA. They killed themselves together.

TOM. I don't want that. I've never felt so alive.

DIANA. Me neither.

TOM. This is inconceivable. You've just jilted one fiance. I'm supposed to be wooing his sister. We're all about to toast each other in champagne...What can we do?

DIANA. We could just run away.

TOM. Now?

DIANA. *(indicating the garden door)* Go out of the door and never come back.

TOM. And leave them to work out what had happened?

DIANA. They never would. They'd think we'd been

kidnapped by terrorists.

TOM. Then they'd spend their lives looking for us. We couldn't do that.

DIANA. Perhaps we could leave them a note?

TOM. Saying what? 'Sorry, Diana's changed her mind again, and I'm actually trying to seduce every woman in the neighbourhood. Be in touch soon.'

DIANA. Are you?

TOM. What?

DIANA. Hoping to seduce me?

TOM. Oh, yes. Oh god, yes.

DIANA. Thank heavens for that. I just needed to be sure.

TOM. Before what?

DIANA. Before causing another holocaust. Before bringing the roof down on our heads. They'll put me in the mad house, you know.

TOM. I won't let them.

DIANA. There's no such thing as love at first sight.

TOM. I thought that too.

DIANA. Can it possibly last?

TOM. It's lasted two hours so far.

DIANA. An eternity.

TOM. I never thought I'd get the chance to speak to you.

DIANA. We might have spent our entire lives wondering.

(paces up and down)

I haven't the slightest...faintest...foggiest idea what to do. I'm engaged to two people already and...Everyone will think I've completely lost my mind.

TOM. Perhaps you should marry all three of us – then at least I'll have one third of you.

DIANA. Would that be enough?

TOM. No. I want every particle of you.

DIANA. Oh God! We don't remotely know each other. What if you discovered I was a monster to be with?

TOM. I'd still love you.

DIANA. What if I discover you're a sexual pervert?

TOM. I'm not.

DIANA. What if...what if it's all a fantasy and we found we hated each other after six months?

TOM. *Then* we'll do the *Romeo and Juliet* thing.

DIANA. How can I explain to Geoff? How can I explain to Jamie? How can you explain to Holly? How do you feel about Holly anyway?

TOM. She's very sweet, but... *(shrugs)*

DIANA. How can we explain to *anybody?* Oh God, it's impossible!

TOM. Yes. Can I...?

DIANA. What?

TOM. Can I kiss you?

DIANA. No.

TOM. Why not?

DIANA. There'd be no going back then.

TOM. There isn't anyway.

DIANA. Isn't there?

TOM. I don't think so. Do you?

DIANA. No. Oh God!

TOM. You've said 'Oh God' three times now.

DIANA. I know, and I don't even believe in God.

TOM. What do you believe in?

DIANA. I don't know. You and me, I think.

TOM. Good. Hang on to that.

DIANA. Oh God!

> *(She buries her face in her hands.* **ANN** *enters with a dish of canapes. Takes in the situation.)*

ANN. *Now* what's happening?

TOM. *(all innocence)* Nothing.

ANN. Doesn't look like nothing. Where's Geoff?

TOM. Er...gone to explain to Diana's parents.

ANN. Shouldn't you be doing that, Diana darling?

DIANA. I didn't feel up to it.

ANN. You don't seem to be up to anything at the moment. Are you sure you're doing the right thing here?

DIANA. Yes, er...no, er...yes.

ANN. Well that doesn't seem very convincing. What has she told you, Tom?

TOM. Er...just that she's having a few nerves about it all.

ANN. Well that's natural. Having two fiances in one day is a bit unnerving, I suppose. Now how many do you suppose we're going to be for dinner? Everyone keeps coming in and out, and nobody seems to know whether they want to be here or not. Tom, are you going to be wandering off to the village again?

TOM. No. I'd love to have dinner.

ANN. Diana, dear, would you like to avoid your parents a bit longer and stay for dinner as my son's ex-fiancee?

DIANA. *(with a glance at* TOM*)* Thank you, Ann, that's very kind of you. I'd like that.

ANN. Which only leaves your present fiance. I suppose I'd better cater for him too in case he feels he'd like to join us.

(JAMIE *and* HOLLY *enter carrying champagne and ice bucket.)*

Ah, here's the champagne.

JAMIE. *(opening a bottle)* Where's Geoff? Fled again?

ANN. Gone to explain to Diana's parents.

JAMIE. I'd love to be a fly on the wall for that! Well now, is this last drinks on the *Titanic*, or toasts to the dawn of a new world?

ANN. It's a good question. Nobody seems too sure.

(JAMIE *pours and* HOLLY *hands round glasses.)*

JAMIE. Well whichever it is, let me be magnanimous. Has everyone got a glass? *(raises his glass)* Then here's to Diana and Geoff. May they be...

DIANA. *(quickly)* I think it's bad luck to have that toast while one of us is absent, Jamie.

JAMIE. *(frowning)* Is it? *(a beat)* Very well. Here's to Holly and Tom...

ANN. That's not a very good idea either, darling. They barely know each other yet.

HOLLY. Thank you, Mother.

JAMIE. Well we have to have a toast to something. I know! *(raises his glass again)* Here's to true love!

ANN. That's better.

ALL. To true love!

(blackout)

ACT TWO

SCENE ONE

*(Three hours later. The room is empty. The sound of laughter and clinking cutlery is heard from the dining room next door. **DIANA** enters. She is still in a daze. She wanders hopelessly, then sits. The telephone rings. She stares at it, not knowing what to do. **ANN** enters.)*

ANN. It's all right, Diana dear, I'll get it.

(answers the phone)

Yes? Oh, it's you, darling. You've heard already – good heavens, how news gets around! Yes, it's true – can you believe it! No, don't ask, just don't ask. Apparently they've both known it all their lives and the rest of us are as blind as bats. No, dear, all the arrangements remain exactly the same, it's just the personnel have changed slightly and I've sacked my astrologist. Well, we're all in a state of shock as you can imagine, but I'll fill you in with the gory details next week. Yes, can you believe it! 'Bye.

*(Replaces the phone. Turns to **DIANA**.)*

Well, just about everyone knows now who needs to know. They're all astounded of course. But if anything it seems to have added a frisson of extra excitement to the proceedings. Extraordinary! I just hope you don't change your minds again, Diana dear, or the world will probably come to an end. *(a beat)* Are you all right?

DIANA. Yes.

ANN. Truly? You've hardly said a word all through dinner. If I may say so, you don't seem at all yourself.

DIANA. No, I'm not really, but don't worry, Ann, I'll…I'll sort myself out eventually.

ANN. Well don't take too long, dear – you've got less than four weeks to do it.

(Leaves. **DIANA** *sits, staring blankly into space. More laughter from next door.* **TOM** *enters. She rises.)*

TOM. You're here...

DIANA. Yes.

TOM. Escaping?

DIANA. Yes.

TOM. From me?

DIANA. From everyone. But especially you.

TOM. Why?

DIANA. I couldn't look at you across the table any longer. You're so beautiful.

TOM. I...

DIANA. They mustn't find us together.

TOM. They think I've gone to the bathroom.

DIANA. I don't know what to do. Oh God, I don't know what to do!

(She weeps. He goes to comfort her. Takes her by the shoulders and holds her. The embrace turns into a kiss. Long and gentle. Finally they break. Silence.)

TOM. Well that's it. No going back now.

DIANA. No. How are we going to tell them? They'll think I'm insane.

TOM. We'll have to. They've changed all the wedding arrangements.

DIANA. They can't change them again! Ann said the world would come to an end.

TOM. So what? It probably will anyway.

DIANA. But how...? Who...? How am I going to explain to Geoff? How are you going to explain to Holly? How can we possibly explain any of it to anybody?

TOM. I think...the only way...is to tell Ann first.

DIANA. Ann?

TOM. Yes. Tell her…and then let her tell the others.

DIANA. I couldn't possibly tell her! She'll refuse to believe it. Or if she does believe it she'll have me certified.

TOM. I'll tell her.

DIANA. You?

TOM. Yes. I'll explain what's happened…as best I can. And then, if she decides to certify anyone at least it will be me.

DIANA. No. No, we can't…

TOM. We have to, my love. The longer we leave it the worse it will be.

DIANA. Oh…

TOM. You go back in there…tell Ann I'm here and I need to speak to her…and whatever you do, don't let any of them follow her in here until we're ready.

DIANA. Are you sure?

TOM. Yes.

DIANA. Do you think you can do it?

TOM. It's the only way.

DIANA. *(fearful)* All right. And then when you've done it…

TOM. Yes?

DIANA. We'll do the *Romeo and Juliet* thing.

TOM. Right. Kiss me again first.

(She does. Then goes. He wanders. The sound of subdued voices next door. Eventually **ANN** *enters.)*

ANN. Tom? Now what is it? I gather you've something to tell me?

TOM. Yes.

ANN. Please – don't tell me that Holly's pregnant. I couldn't take any more shocks today.

TOM. No, no, nothing like that.

ANN. Thank heavens for that!

TOM. It's probably worse than that actually.

ANN. *(after a moment)* I think I'd better sit down.

TOM. Yes.

(*She sits, staring at him. He hesitates.*)

You see, Ann…the thing is…this is going to be hard to believe…but Diana and I have fallen in love.

(*pause*)

ANN. (*eventually*) Diana and you?

TOM. Yes.

ANN. Don't be silly. You've only just met.

TOM. Yes.

ANN. Don't be silly. She's in love with Geoff.

TOM. She loves Geoff. She's not in love with him.

ANN. Don't be silly. There's no such thing as love at first sight.

TOM. That's what we thought.

(*pause*)

ANN. You're telling me…that in the midst of this afternoon's revelations, and reversals, and revolutions…you and Diana took one look at each other, and forgetting all previous affiliations, decided that you wanted only each other, amongst the whole of humanity, for the rest of time, until death do you part?

TOM. Yes.

ANN. You're mad, both of you.

TOM. That's what Diana thought you'd think.

ANN. I do. Why isn't she telling me this herself?

TOM. She didn't dare. She thought you'd think she was mad.

ANN. I do.

TOM. That's what she thought.

ANN. You're both mad.

TOM. Yes, that's what we thought you'd think.

ANN. I do.

TOM. (*nodding*) That's what we thought.

ANN. And what about you and Holly?

TOM. Ditto Diana and Geoff.

ANN. Just like that? It's been fun while it lasted, but now we've found the real thing, thank you and goodbye.

TOM. More or less.

ANN. Oh, my poor Holly. Oh, poor Geoff.

TOM. Yes.

ANN. What are you going to do about them?

TOM. Well…they'll have to know.

ANN. How are you going to tell them?

TOM. That's the thing. We were rather hoping you'd tell them.

ANN. Me?

TOM. Yes.

ANN. Why me?

TOM. You'd do it better than we would.

ANN. But I think you're both mad.

TOM. Perhaps we are – that's why you'd be better at telling them.

(Pause. **ANN** *wipes her brow.)*

ANN. Perhaps it's me that's mad. I go to extraordinary lengths to help organise a hugely elaborate wedding for one of my offspring and his fiancee, only to discover that it's actually going to be for his fiancee and someone who isn't even part of my family, only to be told it's *really* for his fiancee and someone who isn't part of my family and who's a complete stranger to all of us. *Are* you intending to take over the wedding by the way…or whatever it's called now?

TOM. We haven't thought that far.

ANN. Well, you may as well. It's taken you only a matter of minutes to decide you're in love with each other – you've a whole month to prepare for the wedding. And if you wake up tomorrow morning and decide you don't love each other after all, it gives Diana plenty of time to find somebody else.

TOM. I can understand your scepticism. I know it seems unreal. In a way it is – our world has been turned upside down.

ANN. I think the whole universe has been turned upside down! The laws of nature are in total turmoil.

TOM. Yes.

ANN. And I think it's very cowardly of you not to tell them all yourselves.

TOM. Yes.

ANN. But I can see why you wouldn't want to tell them yourselves.

TOM. Yes.

ANN. Is yes the only thing you have to say?

TOM. Yes.

ANN. But even so, surely the right and proper thing to do is to go in there and face them all, and try to explain what's happened…not that you could explain it…not that anyone could explain it…because it's inexplicable. But if they can all make some kind of sense of it then you will obviously have made a better job of it than you've made here with me,

TOM. I couldn't…they wouldn't…it isn't…

ANN. It isn't what?

TOM. It isn't remotely possible…for me in my present state…to be able to even consider…how I would conceivably go about that.

ANN. No, that's evident. So you want me to do it?

TOM. Yes.

ANN. Explain the inexplicable?

TOM. Yes. Please.

ANN. Hm. *(thinks)* Do you think I should tell them all at once, or one at a time?

TOM. I don't know.

ANN. I think it would have to be one at a time. If I told them all at once there might be mass hysteria and riot in the streets.

TOM. Probably.

ANN. And Holly at least deserves to be told in private. As indeed does Geoff.

TOM. Whatever you say.

ANN. And if afterwards one or other of them decides to employ Mafia hitmen and have you castrated, you realise it won't be my doing?

TOM. Quite.

ANN. Right. *(hesitates)* I don't suppose in the midst of this whirlwind romance you've found time to go to bed with each other yet?

TOM. We've barely even kissed.

ANN. You surprise me. You've had most of the afternoon after all. *(a beat)* Well then, first of all I need to talk to Diana.

TOM. Diana?

ANN. Yes. I can't speak to anyone until I've heard her confirm this. I need to assure myself that she's as demented as you are. Ask her to come and see me.

TOM. Right.

(turns to go)

ANN. Discreetly.

TOM. Yes. *(stops again)* I'm usually quite a sane sort of person actually.

ANN. I'll take your word for it.

*(He turns to go. At that moment **GEOFF** enters, almost bumping into him.)*

TOM. Ah.

GEOFF. What's going on?

TOM. Um…

GEOFF. Everyone's going in and out of the dining room looking as if the world is about to end. What's happening, Ann?

ANN. Er – thank you, Tom, you carry on and do as we discussed.

GEOFF. What…?

(TOM leaves. GEOFF turns back to ANN.)

ANN. Geoff dear…I, er…I'm not quite ready to talk to you yet.

GEOFF. Talk to me? What about?

ANN. I need to have a little word with Diana first. Then I'll explain to you. Would you mind very much leaving us alone for a moment?

GEOFF. Diana? What is it? Why can't you tell me now?

ANN. Because I don't know enough myself now, and I need to find out.

GEOFF. Well, it's all very unnerving. Has something happened?

ANN. An awful lot seems to be happening – some of it instigated by you – so could you just be patient a little while longer.

GEOFF. Well, if you say so.

ANN. I'd be grateful. I won't be long.

(He turns. DIANA enters. They look at each other for a moment, then GEOFF leaves. Silence. ANN shakes her head.)

I think I'm dreaming this.

(turns to DIANA)

Tell me I'm dreaming this.

DIANA. No. I'm afraid it's true.

ANN. Has Geoff gone?

DIANA. *(looking behind her)* Yes.

ANN. *(after a moment)* Diana, as well as being beautiful, and warm, and generous, and all those other things, I've always thought of you as a level headed sort of girl. The sort *The Thinker* would be proud of. That's why I was so happy that my Jamie was going to marry you. And then marginally less happy that dear Geoff was going to marry you. Now I discover, after all these years and on virtually the eve of your wedding, that you're actually an adolescent school-girl who not only has her head in the clouds, but her heart in an ice-box and her brain in the food mixer. What has happened to you?

DIANA. I fell in love.

ANN. Literally at first sight?

DIANA. Yes.

ANN. It doesn't happen.

DIANA. That's what I thought.

ANN. It's a mirage, an illusion, a conjurer's trick. You can fall into infatuation, you can fall into sexual obsession, you can fall into a manhole, but you can't fall in love.

DIANA. I did.

ANN. How do you know?

DIANA. You just know. There's no mistaking.

ANN. How do you know it's none of those other things?

DIANA. Infatuation or sexual attraction?

ANN. Or even a manhole.

DIANA. Those things don't even come into the equation... well hardly.

ANN. *(frowning)* What does then?

DIANA. The knowledge that this is it.

ANN. For life?

DIANA. Yes.

ANN. On ten seconds acquaintance?

DIANA. Yes.

ANN. Well...I'm going to see my astrologist never works again. Is there nothing at all I can say that will make you hesitate from this irrevocable step, and just reflect for a while?

DIANA. I can't. We can't. There isn't time. Everyone knows something has happened. We can't hide it.

ANN. We could tell them you've had some sort of brain seizure and have to go into a retreat for a little while.

DIANA. *(smiling)* If I thought that would change anything, I would.

ANN. *(sighing)* Very well. So you want me to break the news to Geoff?

DIANA. I don't think I have the strength to myself.

ANN. And of course to Holly?

DIANA. Same applies.

ANN. Very well. But make no mistake, this won't be just burning all your boats – it'll be setting fire to the Titanic before it sinks.

DIANA. I know.

ANN. Then you'd better go in there and send Geoff back... No, perhaps I should see Holly first...or perhaps I should see them both together...no, that would be too much...Who do you think I should tell first?

DIANA. Um...I think you should tell Geoff first. Then he's got time to come and kill me while you're telling Holly.

ANN. Yes, that sounds a good plan. And who's going to tell poor Jamie?

DIANA. I suppose I'll have to do that. But only once you've told the others.

ANN. I hope he doesn't laugh so hard he has a heart attack.

DIANA. Yes, he might.

(Goes. **ANN** *sits in thought. Shakes her head and sighs.)*

ANN. Jane Austen, eat your heart out!

*(***GEOFF*** *enters.)*

GEOFF. Diana looks as if she's in a trance. What's it all about?

ANN. *(patting the sofa beside her)* Sit down.

GEOFF. Is it that serious?

ANN. I'm not sure whether it's serious or a matter of pure hilarity. You'll have to decide for yourself.

GEOFF. Oh dear.

ANN. How do I begin? Diana...No – Tom...No – you and Diana...*(shakes her head)* I'm at a loss.

GEOFF. For heavens sake, Ann! Put me out of my misery.

ANN. It seems the betrothal situation has changed yet again.

GEOFF. The betrothal situation?

ANN. Yes.

GEOFF. What do you mean?

ANN. Diana – despite originally believing it was Jamie she wanted to marry…and despite having then decided that, no, it was you she wanted to marry…has now decided that it's Tom she wants to marry.

(pause)

GEOFF. Tom?

ANN. Yes.

GEOFF. She doesn't know Tom.

ANN. She's said, 'Hello, pleased to meet you'. Apparently that's enough.

GEOFF. I'm sorry – I don't understand.

ANN. No, it is a bit difficult. I'll try to elucidate. When Diana and Tom met for the first time this afternoon, it seems the earth shook, the moon fell out of the sky, and the planets changed their courses. None of the rest of us noticed at the time, but that's what happened. It was instantaneous, volcanic, nuclear, love at first sight. And so all, um…previous arrangements are, as it were, on hold.

GEOFF. Love at first sight?

ANN. Yes.

GEOFF. There's no such thing.

ANN. That's what I said.

GEOFF. It's a Mills and Boon fiction.

ANN. That's what I thought.

GEOFF. Who told you this?

ANN. Both Tom and Diana. Separately. They appeared to be sincere.

GEOFF. *(indicating next door)* I've just left Diana.

ANN. In a trance, you said.

GEOFF. I put it down to the enormity of what she and I had done. I never imagined...

ANN. It was the enormity of what she and Tom have done.

GEOFF. *(after a moment)* Are you telling me that everything we've been through today – all the agony of my persuading Diana, and confessing to Jamie, and explaining to you, and all the rest of it...was all for nothing?

ANN. Evidently.

GEOFF. I don't know what to say.

ANN. No. I sympathise. *(pause)* I know it must be heart-breaking for you, Geoff – just as I imagine it has been for Jamie – but then maybe you can both console yourselves with the thought that, if Diana's affections are so fickle, then perhaps you're well out of it.

GEOFF. *(shaking his head)* Diana's not like that. I can't believe it.

ANN. Apparently she can hardly believe it herself.

GEOFF. This is why she's been so strange.

ANN. Yes.

GEOFF. It's impossible! Are you saying they're planning on taking over all the wedding arrangements?

ANN. Well, I don't suppose even they are crazy enough to want to move that fast, but the way things are going today...*(shrugs)* Who knows? As it's all laid on, they may decide to throw caution to the winds and take a punt at it.

GEOFF. Surely not. They wouldn't be so insane.

ANN. Certainly the thought of my having to ring up all those people to say that the cast list has changed yet again is something I don't think I could contemplate. The vicar for one would probably abandon the cloth and take to brothel keeping or something.

GEOFF. *(distraught)* Oh God...What am I going to do?

ANN. I'm so sorry, Geoffrey dear. It must be a dreadful shock.

GEOFF. It took every bit of courage I had to do what I did this afternoon...and then when it seemed Diana agreed with me...I was over the moon. I could hardly believe it. Now you're telling me all that was just an illusion?

ANN. I'm not sure what's illusion and what's real any more. But I promised to tell you, so now I have.

GEOFF. Why didn't she tell me?

ANN. She couldn't bring herself to.

(JAMIE *and* HOLLY *enter.*)

JAMIE. Who couldn't bring herself to what?

GEOFF. *(turning away)* Oh, bloody hell!

JAMIE. Mother, what on earth is going on? Everyone keeps appearing and disappearing, Diana and Tom are sitting in there looking as if the Day of Judgement is looming, and nobody will tell us a word about what's happening!

ANN. *(to* GEOFF*)* Will you tell them, or shall I?

GEOFF. You. I wouldn't know how.

HOLLY. What is it, Mother? What's happened?

ANN. What's happened is that Diana and Tom, in the few nanoseconds that they have known each other, have apparently decided that they are madly in love and want each other and only each other to the exclusion of anyone else.

(pause)

JAMIE. Diana and Tom?

ANN. Yes.

HOLLY. They've hardly met.

ANN. Hardly is, it seems, enough.

JAMIE. They're saying it's love at first sight?

ANN. Yes.

HOLLY. There's no such thing.

ANN. They...*(hand to forehead)* I've had this conversation so many times.

JAMIE. Do you accept this, Geoff?

*(**GEOFF** shrugs hopelessly.)*

GEOFF. I'm as flummoxed as you are.

HOLLY. *(to **ANN**)* How do you know all this?

ANN. They both explained it to me, with a great deal of hesitancy, and lack of clarity, and inconsistency...but I'm pretty sure I got the gist of it correctly.

JAMIE. Why did they explain it to you?

ANN. Apparently I was the only one they dared tell it to, face to face. Why they dared tell me, I've no idea. As the jilted prospective mother-in-law I would have thought they'd both be petrified at the idea, but there you are. Telling it to any of you was evidently yet more daunting.

HOLLY. So...let me get this straight, Mother...Diana is now no longer interested in marrying Geoff...and Tom is no longer interested in being with me...and they both want only to be with each other?

ANN. That's right.

*(**HOLLY** sits, on the verge of tears.)*

I'm so sorry, Holly darling. Did you really care for him?

HOLLY. I don't know. I thought I did. But now...

ANN. Now he isn't the person you thought he was.

*(**HOLLY** shakes her head and sits in a coma.)*

JAMIE. Well, this beats everything. I thought Geoff's little bombshell was shattering enough, but this is...well, it's...

ANN. Don't try and find analogies, dear – I've run out of them myself.

*(Silence. Everyone is lost in their own thoughts. **TOM** and **DIANA** enter holding hands. The others all look at them. Long silence. Then they all speak together.)*

ALL. What are you...? Could you please...? Would you like to...? Are we really meant to...?

(They stop. Look at each other. Try again.)

Are you seriously...? Would you please...? What on earth...? Would you like to...?

(They stop again. Silence.)

DIANA. I know how it must seem, everyone. We're completely loony. Especially me. But...well it just happened, and there was nothing we could do about it.

JAMIE. So the last four years we've had together were...a charade...a mirage?

DIANA. No. They were great, Jamie, just...ordinary.

JAMIE. And ordinary isn't good enough for you.

DIANA. Not any more.

GEOFF. And everything we talked about this afternoon – that meant nothing.

DIANA. No, it all made sense, Geoff. It's just that good sense isn't enough any more either.

JAMIE. So ordinary good sense goes out of the window, and fairy-tale fantasy flies in down the chimney?

DIANA. It's no fairy tale. It's for real.

HOLLY. How can it be, Di? You don't know what's real. You don't know anything about each other.

TOM. We know enough.

HOLLY. And you didn't know enough about me?

TOM. No.

HOLLY. Even though we've known each other about a hundred times longer than you've known Diana.

TOM. No.

JAMIE. Well if you ask me you're bonkers, both of you.

DIANA. It must seem that way.

JAMIE. Let's look at this thing objectively.

DIANA. Must we, Jamie?

JAMIE. Yes, I think we must. It's the whole reason I gave you *The Thinker.*

DIANA. Oh, that bloody statue!

JAMIE. There's a lot at stake here. Quite apart from a thundering great wedding that nobody knows who is for yet, or who's going to have to pay for, or who is even eligible to be invited to – there's the small matter of several different people's chances of lifetime happiness involved.

DIANA. That's why we're doing what we're doing.

JAMIE. Twaddle!

TOM. Excuse me, I...

JAMIE. Quiet you.

DIANA. It wouldn't help anyone's chances of happiness if I married the wrong person.

JAMIE. But how do you decide who is the right person, that's the point? Do you take a leap in the dark because you're high as a kite over some passing stranger who chucks a fire bomb into your life? Do you gamble on a roller-coaster ride with an old buddy who waits to propose until you're almost walking down the aisle? Do you hang onto a dear old tried-and-tested, stick-in-the-mud partner who knows you inside out and back to front? You see, when it comes to the crunch, what is actually needed is a cool, carefully assessed, rationally thought out decision on the matter, or you might end up having made a prize balls-up of the whole shebang.

ANN. Very succinctly put, darling.

JAMIE. Are you with me on this, Geoff?

GEOFF. Absolutely.

JAMIE. *(to the statuette)* Are you with me, Thinker? *(disguised voice)* absolutely! *(normal voice)* There you are. Well...?

TOM. Excuse me, I...

JAMIE. Quiet, you. *(to* DIANA*)* Well...?

DIANA. *(at a loss)* I don't...I can't...

JAMIE. Obviously not. Then what we require is some proper procedure here. I'll tell you what we'll do – the three of us will put our cases to you, and to the gathered assembly, in as brief and concise a manner as possible, and then we'll all take a vote on it. What do you say?

DIANA. Don't be ridiculous! I'm not having my love life decided by a majority vote!

JAMIE. Why not? You don't seem to be able to decide it any other way.

DIANA. I've told you – I *have* decided.

JAMIE. But not in any rational manner.

DIANA. It isn't a rational decision. It's a...a...

JAMIE. A what?

DIANA. An emotional one.

JAMIE. Exactly! Pure emotion. And therefore not to be trusted.

DIANA. Well if you can't trust your own emotions, what can you trust?

JAMIE. I've told you – objectivity, rationality, scientific assessment.

DIANA. Scientific...!!

TOM. Excuse me...

JAMIE. Quiet, you!

TOM. No, I bloody well won't be quiet!

JAMIE. *(taken aback)* Oh.

TOM. I'm an interested party here too, in case you'd forgotten! Now all right – you two have both had your noses put out of joint in this – I sympathise. I can understand how you feel. But this wasn't something Diana and I planned, just in order to rain on your parade. This was a seismic event that took us both by surprise, and over which we had no control. Me as much as Diana – and I'm as much a believer in logic as you are. But as she says, this is not something that can be decide by mathematical evaluation.

GEOFF. Well, I think it needs to be decided by some sort of evaluation.

HOLLY. Exactly. It hasn't been considered in any shape or form so far.

TOM. Yes, it has.

DIANA. We've considered it.

JAMIE. But not while you've been in a sane and sober state of mind – that's our point. Now I say again – let the three of us put our arguments – and let everyone judge. At the very least it will help to clarify matters. And if Geoff and I are voted out then at least we'll have no more grounds for protest.

DIANA. Well...

JAMIE. I'll go first.

DIANA. *(resigned)* Very well. It's a pointless exercise, but...

JAMIE. Hear me out. What I offer you, Diana, is certainty. Tried and tested over a lifetime of acquaintance and four years of being together. We know each other's innermost secrets – we're happy together in all weathers – we laugh at the same inane jokes – we don't fight over the washing up – we've agreed on what is the best toothpaste – we know each other's erogenous zones – excuse me, Mother... (ANN *closes her eyes.)* No hidden surprises – what you see is what you get. Do you agree?

DIANA. Yes.

JAMIE. Therefore I'm what my father would call your blue chip investment – track record, well insured, steady growth, Bank of England guarantee. No boom-and-bust. And that's what you want in a marriage.

DIANA. Thank you, Jamie.

JAMIE. Geoff. Your turn.

GEOFF. Must I?

JAMIE. If you wish to stake your claim.

GEOFF. Very well. I said it all before – Jamie offers you certainty, I offer you excitement. Every day will be a new day of challenge and anticipation. You won't know what the evening might bring, let alone who'll do the washing up. You won't know which country you'll be living in, let alone which toothpaste to use. You might feel insecure sometimes but you'll never be bored. You might be apprehensive about the future, but you'll never regret the past. And for me your whole body is one great erogenous zone.

ANN. *(closing her eyes again)* Oh.

GEOFF. Sorry, Ann. There – that's all I have to say.

DIANA. Thank you, Geoff.

JAMIE. Tom.

TOM. I can't.

JAMIE. You must. Otherwise everyone will take it you've no case to offer.

(**TOM** *takes* **DIANA**'s *face in his hands and kisses her.*)

DIANA. *(sighing)* Ohhh.

TOM. That's my case.

(Pause. Finally **JAMIE** *nods.)*

JAMIE. O.K. Fair enough.

GEOFF. Is that it? We're asking everyone to judge on a kiss?

JAMIE. Well, we've done all we can. It's old hat versus new hormones. I suggest we go to the vote.

HOLLY. It's a ridiculous vote!

JAMIE. Why?

HOLLY. Those two aren't involved in it. You and Geoff will vote for yourselves. I'm hardly a disinterested party. That only leaves Mother!

JAMIE. All right – Mother, you and Thinker have the casting vote. What do you say?

ANN. I say that the whole thing is a farce, and I wouldn't vote for any one of you at this stage.

JAMIE. Oh.

GEOFF. So much for that exercise.

ANN. However I think you're missing the point.

JAMIE. What's that?

ANN. It's not our vote you should be considering. It's Diana's. After all, hers is the only vote that matters. Diana dear, with your most sensible hat on, and having heard the arguments from the various proposing parties, how do you feel about everything now?

DIANA. *(after a moment)* I don't know...I can't...I just...

(She is lost for words. ANN shrugs hopelessly.)

GEOFF. You see – she hasn't a clue.

JAMIE. Well then, I have one final suggestion.

DIANA. Oh heavens! What now, Jamie?

JAMIE. No, this seems to me a sensible one. All right, you know what I'm offering. You have a pretty good idea of what Geoff is offering. You haven't the faintest idea what Tom is offering. Has she, Tom – be fair?

TOM. No.

JAMIE. I therefore suggest that you go off with him for a week – somewhere of your own choosing, far from us and the madding crowd – and you find out about each other. You discover whether you quarrel over the washing up, and what kind of toothpaste to use, and where your erogenous zones are – sorry, Mother – and then you come back, and we'll have this conversation again. And if you are still of the same opinion, then Geoff and I will accept it – no further argument. What do you say, Geoff?

GEOFF. Sounds reasonable.

JAMIE. Tom?

TOM. Yes, that suits me. *(to DIANA)* What do you say?

DIANA. I...

JAMIE. Can you take a week off work, both of you?

TOM. I could fix it.

JAMIE. Diana?

DIANA. Probably.

JAMIE. Well, if they fire you both, what the hell – it's only a job compared to the rest of your lives.

ANN. At last! A sensible suggestion from somebody.

DIANA. When would we go?

JAMIE. The sooner it takes place, the better. How about now?

TOM. Now?

JAMIE. Well there's no point mooning around here any longer. You'll miss out on the coffee and brandy and Mother's amazing home-made petit-fours, but the sooner you embark on this voyage of exploration the sooner you'll know if you are peas in a pod, or chalk and cheese. Wouldn't you say?

(DIANA *and* TOM *look at each other.*)

DIANA. Yes.

TOM. Yes.

HOLLY. Where will they go?

JAMIE. Up to them.

GEOFF. I know a great little place…

JAMIE. Thank you, Geoff – I'm sure Tom knows a few great little places of his own.

TOM. Yes.

HOLLY. But it's dark already.

JAMIE. Well they're fishing in the dark anyway, so it won't make any difference, will it? All they need is to find a bed for the first night – and if their passion is so overwhelming I imagine any old bed will do – and then they can take their time over deciding where to go for the rest of the week.

GEOFF. First big test. They might have their first marital row over it.

JAMIE. Exactly. They might even bust up over it.

ANN. I'll save some Sunday lunch, just in case they do. All right you two?

DIANA. Yes.

TOM. Yes.

ANN. Then collect your things and off you go. Goodbye, Tom. It's been quite an experience meeting you. I don't know if we'll ever see you again, but I'm sure we're leaving Diana in good hands, for one week at any rate.

TOM. Thank you for...well everything. You're a great family.

JAMIE. Yes, we know.

TOM. Goodbye, Holly. I'm sorry I didn't give you...quite what you expected.

HOLLY. *(shrugging)* Easy come, easy go.

DIANA. Thank you, boys. I'm so sorry about...I wish I didn't...I hope I haven't...

GEOFF. *(to* **JAMIE***)* Has she managed to finish a single sentence all day?

JAMIE. Don't think so.

GEOFF. Totally indecisive woman. Don't know what we saw in her.

JAMIE. No. Good riddance really.

DIANA. *(smiling)* 'Bye.

*(***TOM*** and* **DIANA** *leave. Pause. Everyone looks at each other.)*

ANN. Well...!

HOLLY. What do we do now?

ANN. I think I need to consult my astrologist.

JAMIE. Don't you dare!

ANN. Well, what do we do?

JAMIE. I don't know.

GEOFF. We can't just sit around for a week. The suspense would be intolerable.

JAMIE. Do you think they'll last that long?

GEOFF. A week?

JAMIE. Yes.

GEOFF. Dunno. Do you?

JAMIE. Dunno. Mother?

ANN. I'll tell you this. It'll be quite a test.

JAMIE. Test?

ANN. Oh yes. To spend a whole week together, with just each other for company, when you know nothing whatsoever about each other – it won't be all wine and roses, I can promise you.

HOLLY. That's true.

JAMIE. Tell you what – let's place bets on it. I'll open a book.

HOLLY. What do you mean?

JAMIE. I'll give you all odds on what happens, and you can place your bets.

GEOFF. Who'll decide the odds?

JAMIE. I will. My risk, my odds. Let me see…Three to one, they're back within three days. Five to one, they last the week. Ten to one, they return having decided to get married.

ANN. Married?

JAMIE. Yes.

ANN. You mean we've got to keep all the wedding arrangements open in case they decide to marry?

HOLLY. They couldn't do that in such a short time.

JAMIE. Why not? Diana's broken off two engagements in an afternoon – surely she can pull off another marriage in a week. Right – ten pound minimum stakes – who's going to have a bet?

HOLLY. You've left out the other runners. What odds on her deciding to come back to you? Or to Geoff?

JAMIE. Good point. *(thinks)* I'll give the same odds as her marrying him. Ten to one. Who'll bet? Mother?

ANN. I couldn't be so frivolous over such a serious subject.

JAMIE. Well you must have some opinion on which of us she'll eventually choose?

ANN. I haven't the slightest idea. Her thought processes are beyond me. I'll leave you to your games. I'm going to have to go and telephone your father again. I expect this time it might bring down the government.

(She goes out.)

GEOFF. Don't know why she's calling him – he has no interest in it any more really.

JAMIE. Oh, that's just her excuse. It won't be Father she's calling, it'll be her astrologist.

GEOFF. I thought she was sacking him?

JAMIE. Never. The worse his forecasts are, the more she relies on him. Right – Holly?

HOLLY. What?

JAMIE. Who do you say Diana will choose?

HOLLY. *(thoughtfully)* I think she'll return to common sense and pick Geoff.

JAMIE. Do you want to bet on that?

HOLLY. No.

JAMIE. Geoff?

GEOFF. I think she'll be so traumatised by the whole business that she'll come back to what she knows best, and choose you.

HOLLY. *(to JAMIE)* And what do you think?

JAMIE. I think she'll decide to leave the country, and end up marrying a Russian billionaire and living in Monte Carlo.

GEOFF. That wasn't among the options.

JAMIE. Nothing she's done all day had been among the options. Why should she change now?

HOLLY. Might be the best solution – as long as the billionaire recompenses us for all the wedding costs and everything. Interesting though…

GEOFF. What?

HOLLY. No-one has bet on her marrying Tom.

JAMIE. Hm.

GEOFF. Mm.

(pause)

JAMIE. *(to the statuette)* Who do you vote for, Thinker?

(silence)

(The lights slowly dim.)

SCENE TWO

(Four weeks later.)

*(**DIANA** stands in the middle of the room in her slimline wedding dress, looking at herself in the mirror.)*

ANN. *(off)* Just coming, Diana dear.

DIANA. No hurry.

*(**ANN** enters dressed for the wedding. She carries a needle and thread.)*

ANN. Here we are. Let me see that hem.

DIANA. It's perfect, Ann. You don't need to fuss.

*(**ANN** kneels beside her to stitch the hem.)*

ANN. It just needs a tiny stitch. Try and keep still, dear – this is quite delicate. *(sews)* You're very wise to walk over to the church from here. This would crease up in a car like nobody's business.

DIANA. Yes.

ANN. Extraordinary, the change in you.

DIANA. Change?

ANN. In the past four weeks you've gone from being a complete mad woman to being the calmest one amongst us all.

DIANA. That's because I finally made the right decision.

ANN. Well, you'll be glad to know my astrologist agrees with you.

DIANA. Oh dear – now I'm worried again.

ANN. Please, don't you start. He charges a fortune, he must get *some* things right. You haven't talked about it much though, Diana. How *did* you decide?

DIANA. One day I'll tell you.

*(**HOLLY** enters, also dressed for the wedding.)*

HOLLY. Oh, Di – you look wonderful! Not long to go. Your father's just rung to say he'll soon be leaving to come over.

DIANA. Good.

HOLLY. And your mother says, stay calm, watch the church gratings with your high heels, and check your panty line isn't showing.

DIANA. She's the most nervous of everybody.

HOLLY. Well, everyone was dreading the wedding, but now it's here it's all very exciting really.

ANN. Who was dreading it?

HOLLY. Well we know you weren't, Mother – it's all done mostly for your benefit.

ANN. I beg your pardon!

HOLLY. Never mind – I'm so glad we didn't have to cancel it.

ANN. So am I, after all that.

DIANA. It's been such an ordeal for you all. I'm so sorry.

ANN. I won't deny it's been a bit stressful, my dear. Having to keep three different guest lists on hold, nearly a hundred people waiting to hear whether they were invited or not, and a room full of presents marked 'Don't open until authorised'!

HOLLY. Not a bad way to choose a husband though. I think no-one should be allowed to get married until they've had at least three different proposals. It would make them all think seriously about it, and probably halve the divorce rate.

ANN. Is that what you're intending to do? In which case count me out. You'll have to organise your own wedding.

HOLLY. Tell me, Di – how did you *really* decide in the end? Did you mark them all out of a hundred, or did you just draw straws?

DIANA. One day I'll tell you.

(**JAMIE** *sticks his head in. He is dressed in wedding tails and doing up his tie.*)

JAMIE. Am I allowed to peek? It's not bad luck or anything?

ANN. Jamie, dear, you should be at the church. You can't arrive after Diana!

JAMIE. Don't worry, I'll be there. Just wanted to check everything's in order. *(to* **DIANA***)* You look wonderful.

DIANA. Thank you.

JAMIE. Are you all right, old thing?

DIANA. Yes, my darling, I'm fine.

JAMIE. No second thoughts...sorry, third...sorry, fourth or fifth thoughts?

DIANA. None at all.

JAMIE. Thank God for that! *(They kiss.)* I love you.

DIANA. I love you too.

JAMIE. And strange to relate, I think you made the right choice.

DIANA. So do I.

JAMIE. Although I'm still in the dark as to how you decided.

DIANA. One day I'll tell you.

JAMIE. Yes, well, I'll...

(As he turns to go, **GEOFF** *looks in, also in tails.)*

Ah. Look who else is here.

GEOFF. Don't know if it's allowed or not.

ANN. Not strictly speaking, Geoff, but nowadays there seems no such thing as protocol.

GEOFF. Just wanted to be sure she was all right. *(admires* **DIANA***)* Oh my God! So lovely.

DIANA. Thank you.

GEOFF. I want to cry.

DIANA. Save it for the church.

GEOFF. Am I allowed a kiss before you get there? Or is that stretching protocol too far?

DIANA. No, you can kiss me.

HOLLY. Just don't smudge her lipstick.

(They kiss.)

GEOFF. I knew you'd decide right in the end.

DIANA. If there is ever such a thing as a right decision.

GEOFF. Well there may not be, but for God's sake don't go back on it now.

DIANA. *(smiling)* I won't.

GEOFF. How did you, by the way?

DIANA. Decide?

GEOFF. Yes.

DIANA. One day I'll tell you.

GEOFF. *Very* unsatisfactory.

JAMIE. She won't tell anyone.

DIANA. It's...personal.

JAMIE. You can't keep it personal from your own husband!

DIANA. Well, once he's my husband I might let him know. It'll be too late for him to pull out then, won't it?

GEOFF. Very unsatisfactory.

DIANA. *(smiling)* I love you.

GEOFF. I love you too.

DIANA. See you there.

GEOFF. Yes. *(to* **JAMIE***)* Come on, you.

JAMIE. Right.

> *(***TOM** *enters, dressed similarly.)*

God, it's like a penguin parade in here. What are you doing here?

TOM. I was invited – thanks to everyone's generosity.

JAMIE. Yes, but don't take advantage of it. No-one's supposed to see her before the church.

TOM. Then what are you doing here?

JAMIE. I live here – I have special dispensation.

TOM. And Geoff?

GEOFF. I practically live here – it counts the same.

TOM. Well, am I not allowed to visit?

DIANA. Yes, Tom, you're allowed. Come in.

> *(He comes forward and stares at her.)*

TOM. Oh my God! You look stunning.

DIANA. Thank you.

TOM. If I'd known you were going to look like this on your wedding day...

DIANA. You what?

TOM. I'd have used different tactics right from the start.

JAMIE. Too late. What's done is done. You can't alter the order of things now.

TOM. No. *(to* **DIANA***)* Can I...?

DIANA. What?

TOM. Kiss you.

ANN. Well everyone else has, so why not you?

DIANA. Yes, please.

(They kiss.)

JAMIE. Touching.

GEOFF. They'd have made quite a good couple.

JAMIE. Yeh. Wouldn't have lasted though.

GEOFF. Not a chance. Chalk and cheese.

JAMIE. Flash in the pan.

HOLLY. Shut up you lot. Get off to the church.

ANN. Has whoever's meant to have the ring, got the ring?

GEOFF. Ring? What ring?

JAMIE. Search me.

GEOFF. Did I give it to you?

JAMIE. No, I gave it to you.

DIANA. Oh, go away you two, before I change my mind again and call off the whole thing.

JAMIE. She would too.

GEOFF. Better go. You coming, Tom?

TOM. Won't be long. There's just something I need to say to Diana.

JAMIE. Don't try and alter her decision. It's too late for that.

TOM. No, I won't.

GEOFF. And there's no point asking her how she decided. She's not telling.

TOM. Right.

(They go.)

HOLLY. Is this private? Do you want Mum and I to leave?

TOM. No, it's all right.

ANN. Well I'm not sure that I want to hear. And I have to get my very expensive hat on anyway, so I'm going upstairs. The dress is fine now, Diana.

DIANA. Thank you, Ann. For everything.

ANN. Well it's been a bumpy ride, but we got there in the end. You're an astonishing girl, Diana. Strange way of going about things but you seem to end up in the right place eventually. I'm very happy for you.

DIANA. Thank you.

ANN. And if it doesn't work out – well at least we'll have got this wretched wedding out of the way.

(ANN goes. HOLLY looks from TOM to DIANA.)

HOLLY. I think, um…I think I'll go too. I'll fetch your bouquet, Diana.

(DIANA nods. HOLLY leaves. TOM takes DIANA's hands.)

TOM. I'm sorry I put you through such hell.

DIANA. It was worth it.

TOM. Probably the only way to find out about each other.

DIANA. Yes.

TOM. A lifetime condensed into one week.

DIANA. Almost.

TOM. Even so – it's not too late to change your mind.

DIANA. Why would I do that?

TOM. It's not too late right up to the moment you say, 'I do.' What matters is to be right.

DIANA. It's right.

TOM. Just thought I'd say it. You're a terrific girl.

DIANA. You're not so bad yourself.

TOM. See you in church.

DIANA. Yes.

(He starts to go, then stops.)

TOM. Have you told anyone what happened?

DIANA. *(shaking her head)* One day I might.

(He grins and goes. She waits. **HOLLY** *returns with the bouquet.)*

HOLLY. Nearly time. Your father will be here soon.

DIANA. Yes.

HOLLY. Are you all right?

DIANA. I've never been better in my life.

HOLLY. Well that must be a good omen.

DIANA. Yes.

HOLLY. I mean...

DIANA. What?

HOLLY. Well, after all that you can't be *totally* sure you chose right.

DIANA. I am.

HOLLY. How?

DIANA. Because I found myself.

HOLLY. During that week away?

DIANA. Mhm.

HOLLY. Won't you at least tell *me* what happened?

DIANA. Do you really want to know? After...

HOLLY. Oh, it's all right, I'm over him now. Tell me.

DIANA. Well...You must promise not to tell anyone else.

HOLLY. I promise.

DIANA. It was a close run thing, Holly.

HOLLY. *(eager)* What happened?

DIANA. The first night was disaster.

HOLLY. Oh...

DIANA. It was too late to get where we were going, and we stopped at a B & B. Cold and dark – horrible. There were twin beds in the room. We hadn't a thing to say to each other. We went to bed and barely said goodnight.

HOLLY. Ohh...

DIANA. Next day we got to the hotel Tom knew. Pretty enough, but the weather was awful and we were both still shell-shocked. We mooned about all afternoon, and then had a dreadful row over dinner.

HOLLY. What about?

DIANA. Politics.

HOLLY. Good Lord!

DIANA. We went to bed without touching each other. Next day I was in tears for most of the time, and Tom was black as thunder. That evening we had another row.

HOLLY. What about?

DIANA. Religion.

HOLLY. You can't be serious!

DIANA. This went on for three days, and then we decided to call it all off and come home. On the way we were having another huge row – this time about whether I should marry Jamie or Geoff. And in the middle of the row Tom drove into a ditch and nearly turned the car over.

HOLLY. Oh!

DIANA. And then as we were waiting for a garage to come and tow us out of the ditch, the sun suddenly came out and we looked around and realised we were in the middle of the most beautiful countryside. Tom said let's climb to the top of that hill. So we did, and we lay on the top with the whole of Dorset laid out below us, and Tom said he was sick to death of treating me like some...unattainable goddess. And I said I was sick to death of being treated like one. And he said, then why did I behave like one? And I said, I don't but everyone just treats me like one. And he said, well I'm not treating you like one any more. And he leant over and kissed me...and...and...

HOLLY. Yes?

DIANA. He made love to me there and then on top of the hill.

HOLLY. Ohhh…

DIANA. And then we went back to the hotel, and he made love to me all during the next three days and nights…

HOLLY. Ohhh…

DIANA. And in between we talked and talked, and…well he's everything I knew he was, Holly. And I fell in love all over again.

HOLLY. Oh…

DIANA. You see, I've known you all so long…I've always behaved as you expected me to behave…so I've never really found out…who I was.

HOLLY. Ah.

DIANA. And then, for the first time in my life…I was able to open up and be myself. *(nods)* Yes, that's it…with him I am myself.

HOLLY. Ah.

DIANA. And so finally, on the way back home, when we were stuck in a traffic jam on the M3, he said, 'I know it's daft, but will you marry me?' And of course I said yes. And here we are.

HOLLY. Ohhh. I think *I'm* going to cry.

DIANA. And, as your mother says, if it doesn't work out – well at least we'll be done with this bloody wedding.

HOLLY. I'm sure it will. It just shows – first instincts can be right. It just takes time for them to explain themselves.

DIANA. I'm so sorry for all I've done…to you…and Geoff…

HOLLY. Oh, don't worry about us. I might even marry Geoff myself.

(**DIANA** *raises her eyebrows.*)

DIANA. You haven't spent a Yorkshire weekend with him too, have you?

HOLLY. No, but I'm working on it.

(They smile at each other. There is the sound of a car outside.)

That'll be your dad.

DIANA. Tell him I'll be straight out.

*(**HOLLY** hands her the bouquet.)*

HOLLY. Good luck. I'll be right behind you.

*(Goes. **DIANA** checks herself in the mirror. Notices* The Thinker. *She picks him up, kisses him, drops him in the wastebasket, and leaves.)*

(curtain)

COSTUMES

Two casual outfits and a formal wedding outfit for each character. Coats for Holly and Tom. Wedding dress for Diana.

PROPERTIES

ACT ONE, SCENE ONE

Telephone
Miniature statuette of Rodin's 'Thinker' (aprox 25 cm high)
Weekend case for Tom
Bowl or raspberries and gardening gloves for Ann
Waste basket

SCENE TWO

Tray of glasses for Ann
Dish of canapés for Ann
Champagne bottle for Jamie
Ice bucket for Holly

ACT TWO, SCENE ONE

No further props

SCENE TWO

Sewing kit for Ann
Bouquet for Holly

www.ingramcontent.com/pod-product-compliance
Lightning Source LLC
Chambersburg PA
CBHW070639120726
47909CB00004B/1507